SPEAKING

Greek

A FOREIGN EXCHANGE SERIES BOOK ONE

D1372558

SELENA
LAURENCE

Author's Notes

While the State Hermitage Museum in St Petersburg, Russia does house one of Degas' dancer paintings, it is not L'etoile, as described in this story. L'etoile is owned by a private collection. I used artistic license slipping one of Monsieur Degas' most famous paintings into the collection of one of the world's most famous museums.

The island of Georgios is fictitious. While there are some uninhabited islands in Greece, which bear Georgios as part of their name, the Georgios described in the book is a combination of several real islands, and was used in order to create the setting necessary for the book. Similarly, I have based Greek family relations and culture on real life, but mixed and matched things to fit the story. I'm very grateful to everyone who has traveled to Greece or has Greek heritage and advised me for this book. You all were tremendously helpful, and any errors are entirely my own.

Dedication

To all the travelers, those who do it for money, those who do it for fun, and most of all, those who do it to learn—about the world they live in, and the world beyond.

"The life you have led doesn't need to be the only life you have."

-Anna Quindlen

PROLOGUE

Dear Ms. Richardson:

The staff of the Foreign Studies department at Chicago University is pleased to inform you that you have been accepted to Junior year abroad to study in Georgios, Greece. As part of your financial aid package you will be working twenty hours each week in the accounting department of Stephanos Shipping, in addition to taking classes at American University Georgios.

In order to prepare for your year as a foreign exchange student we require that you attend an orientation on July twenty-second in the conference room of the Foreign Studies department. We also require that you join the Yahoo! group, *ForeignXChange*, where you will be able to interact with the other five students in this year's program.

Enclosed please find all the details regarding your trip, accommodations, internship and classes.

Sincerely,
Anna Gomez
Foreign Exchange Coordinator

CHAPTER ONE

Tess

ForeignXChange Group

Tess: Hey everyone! I'm Tess, and I'll be going to Greece tomorrow. Wanted to introduce myself—I'd love to hear where all of you are going, what classes you're taking, if you're working.

Ciao! (Sorry, I don't know how to say goodbye in Greek)

I'm standing at the edge of the ship, the breeze whipping my blonde hair into knots, while the people on board shout in different languages, clamoring to gather their belongings before we disembark. I recognize some French, and a little German, also Italian, but there are about a dozen other things being bantered around that sound completely foreign. Which, well, since they're called foreign languages makes sense I guess.

The water below me is the bluest blue I've ever seen. I'm used to Lake Michigan, a sort of green or gray, depending on the time of year and the time of day. This water is achingly, cinematically blue. Something you'd see on a Discovery Channel show about aquatic life, or the coral reefs, or marine-based eco-tourism. The ship slowly edges its way up to the dock, and I gather my two suitcases, struggling to balance them on my shoulders.

The ship is a madhouse and I'm only five foot two, so I'm in danger of being mowed over by the enthusiastic crowd. I try to use the two-ton bags hanging off of my shoulders to buffer me from the virtual mosh pit that's formed at the exit down the gangplank.

I'm doing pretty well, having settled in between a tall man with a toddler in his arms on one side and a little old lady on the other. But right as we're about to reach the pavement of the dock the guerilla grandma sees her family who are standing ten feet away yelling and waving like lunatics. She starts shouting back at them in Greek and with a determination I've never seen on someone that old she puts both elbows out, tucks her head, and charges like a defensive lineman taking out a running back. She manages to clip me in the rib cage, and my bag swings back, then forward, gaining momentum that propels me the last two feet off the edge of the gangplank.

I fly onto the sidewalk, and land on my feet, but the bags are heavy and they're still moving even though

I'm trying to stop, so I stumble. Their weight is pulling me down, I'm heading for a horrible impact on solid concrete, when out of nowhere, a pair of hands catch me under the elbows, lifting me, bags and all, upright onto my feet. I stand for a moment trying to catch my breath. Then I look up—way up—to thank whoever has saved me from both humiliation and I'm sure a good deal of pain.

I stare at him blankly, my heart beating erratically as I take in his tan skin, crystalline eyes, and dark, nearly black, wavy hair. He's wearing a blue t-shirt, fitting close in all the right places, and a pair of athletic shorts with beat up Nikes. The stubble that grazes his jaw is the absolute right amount—not too heavy, not too sparse—he must be one of those special one-in-a-million guys blessed with perfect facial hair. My brother, Nate, always talks about how much he hates those guys. Nate can't grow decent stubble to save his life.

A smile spreads across his face and his teeth are as perfect as the rest of him. White, straight, and shiny.

"You okay?" he asks, a slight accent to his English.

I swallow. Hard. Words seem to be escaping me. I don't think I've ever seen a more perfect-looking guy. Ever.

"Did you hit your head or something?" he asks, a small furrow appearing in his brow as he peers at me.

"Oh! No." My brain finally catches up to my libido and I work to get words out of my dropped jaw. "No, I'm fine. Thank you. For catching me, I mean."

He chuckles and raises an eyebrow obviously thinking I'm an idiot. "Sure thing. Old Mrs. Yanos is a vicious one when she wants to get to her grandkids."

That snaps me out of it and I look past him trying to find the ancient battering ram who nearly laid me out.

"Mrs. Yanos? She's dangerous as hell. Can't she read?" I point to the signs written in several languages that say: *Please disembark in an orderly fashion. Safety first.*

Perfect guy looks at me for a minute then busts up laughing.

"What?" I ask, incensed that he's ridiculing me when I've just escaped what surely would have been a life-threatening injury. Well, ok, *could* have been a life-threatening injury. Maybe.

"No one's read that sign or followed the rules in fifty years or so. In fact, I work across the street and I'm here all the time and I don't think I've ever noticed that sign."

"Well what the hell is the point of having rules if no one is going to follow them?"

He shrugs. "Someone probably thought it was a good idea to put it up, but as a *suggestion.* Because everyone knows that Stefan, who captains the ship, doesn't like to dock here since it's got a view of his ex-girlfriend's house, so if you want to get off the ship you have to do it fast or he'll leave again and you'll get stuck going to the far side of the island. Then you've got to call a cab to come get you. It can take a couple of hours all together."

I stare at him again, but this time it's not in lust, it's in disgust. My father is a district attorney and my brother is an FBI agent. My mom was a State police officer until she had us and decided to stay home and consult with the local police department instead. I'm majoring in forensic accounting. We're in law enforcement, and we follow the laws, the rules, and the procedures. I mean, if you don't, society falls apart. Right?

"Again. What's the point of the sign then?" I huff.

He shakes his head. "You've never been to Greece, have you?"

"Nooo…"

"Well, princess, Greece is chill. We don't fuss over the rules too much here. It all works out fine."

Princess? Don't fuss over the rules too much? I sputter, "W-what? You're kidding, right?"

He laughs. Yes, laughs. "Can I get you a valium or something?" he asks. "I don't want you to stroke out here on the docks."

Oh my God. He is such an utter ass. I should have known. Anyone that pretty must be a jerk too. It's a law of nature or something. They get by on their looks, so they learn they can act like an asshole and still skate by.

"Listen," I say, getting as far up in his face as I can, which really isn't all that far since the top of my head barely makes it to his shoulder. So, really I'm getting up in his chest, which, wow, is such a nice chest. I breathe in and smell the ocean, and soap and guy. My head swims a little and I blow out the breath, taking a step back because, shit. *Focus.*

"I don't know who you are, and I'm not an expert on Greece, but it's the source of our modern democratic systems of government, so I don't believe for one moment that no one here follows rules or laws—" Just then a tall, lithe Mediterranean-looking girl appears in front of me. "Excuse me, are you Tess Richardson?" she asks.

I turn to look at her. She's very beautiful, curly shoulder-length hair, big dark eyes, and full lips.

"Yes!" I'm so happy to see this girl even though I don't know her. "You must be Cass."

"I am," she answers, grinning. My new roommate. I'm so happy to see a friendly face. Mr. Perfect did a good job of saving my bacon, but I'd almost rather have wiped out on the pavement he's pissed me off so much now.

"It's so nice to meet you," I say, throwing chill guy a dirty look before I give Cass my most winning smile.

I can see the gorgeous hunk of rule-defying man smirking out of the corner of my eye.

Cass glances at him then does a double-take. *Yeah*, I want to say, *he really is that perfect.*

"So are you ready to go?" She looks between us, obviously confused if he's with me. He's got his arms crossed now, biceps bulging all sexy irritating, and is leaning back against the railing that runs alongside the dock.

"Yes. Definitely." I turn to him. "Thank you for helping me off the ship," I say. God, I sound like a nerd.

He grins and slides a pair of Oakleys on his face. "Anytime, princess."

I grit my teeth. I've known him for all of three minutes and he's given me a nickname. Who does that?

"Let's go," I say to Cass without opening my mouth.

She stares at me and blinks. "Oh-kay then."

I lift my bags higher on my shoulders and look at *perfection* one last time. Too bad he's so annoying.

"Nice to have met you," I say as I step away to follow Cass.

"You never actually met me," he says, still lounging against the railing. "You never got my name," he calls as I walk further away.

"There's a reason for that," I call back without turning around.

The last sound I hear is him laughing as we leave the dock and make our way to Cass's little car.

**

The streets of Georgios are narrow and the Toyota Aygo we're driving in is too. Cass maneuvers it like a grand prix driver, and we lurch around street corners, through tunnels that go underneath buildings, and even onto a curb or two.

"Whoa," I say as she cuts across the corner of a sidewalk at an intersection so that she can get around a delivery truck that's stopped in the dead center of the road. My eyes scan the area for police. "Aren't you worried you'll get a ticket?"

She laughs. "Driving here is a lot different than driving back home."

Cass's been here since the middle of last school year, so she knows what's going on. She's from Chicago University too but I don't remember ever seeing her around campus. She'll be staying until the Christmas holiday then going back home to finish up her final semester.

"But surely they have traffic laws."

"Yeah, but they don't enforce them much. It all works out fine." She brakes as a kid on a bike pulls out into the road without even looking.

I grip the edge of the seat underneath me. What is with everyone here? Has the sun addled all their brains?

"Oh yeah?" I ask. "Like that kid nearly getting killed?"

"Eh, he's fine," she scoffs. As we pull up next to him she leans out the window and says something to him in Greek. The kid grins and shouts something back as he takes off on the bike again.

"So welcome to Greece!" she says out of the blue.

"Thanks." I give her a grateful smile.

"And how did you end up with Niko?" she asks.

"Who?"

"Niko. The guy you were talking to at the dock?"

"Oh. He caught me when this little old woman plowed into me coming down the gangplank of the ship. With my suitcases hanging off of my shoulders I'm like a weeble about to topple over."

"Nicely done," she purrs.

"What do you mean?"

She shakes her head like I'm hopeless. "Niko is the hottest guy on the island. If you ask me, he's the hottest guy for like five islands in any direction. And he doesn't go around helping people for the hell of it. He must have liked you."

The car veers to the left and we start on a winding road that goes up the side of a steep hill.

I snort. "I don't think so. I sort of fell into him, he didn't really have a choice."

"Oh, there's always a choice for Niko. Life is full of choices when your dad is a billionaire."

"Really? Wow. That must be…just wow."

"Right?" She pulls up to the front of a tall, narrow stucco building with a darling little Juliet balcony draped in red carnations. She turns to me as she switches off the ignition. "Ari Stephanos is the wealthiest man in Greece, and Niko is the only heir. All the looks, all the money. He was even a star soccer player at the University of Miami when he went there."

My heart stutters for a moment. "That guy is Ari Stephanos's son? Like Stephanos Shipping?"

"Yep. That's where the billions come from."

I groan. "Ugh. This is so my luck."

Cass gets out of the car and I follow. "What's the problem?" she asks, opening the tiny hatch so I can get my luggage. I hoist one bag out and she wiggles her fingers for me to hand it to her.

"I've got an internship with Stephanos Shipping. I'm supposed to start in their accounting section on Monday."

Cass laughs as she helps me arrange my other bag on my shoulder. "Well, you've already made an impression on your new boss then."

"The boss's son, you mean," I correct. "And I'll probably never see either of them anyway. I'm sure the CEO's office wing is nowhere near my intern desk."

Cass looks at me with sympathy. "Oh, you poor thing. You're right that Niko's high up in the company, but he's not in the CEO's offices. He's the CFO, the head of finance. He really is your new boss."

Perfect. Absolutely perfect.

CHAPTER TWO

Niko

ForeignXChange Group

Kellie: Hi Tess! I'm Kellie and I'm going to Ireland. I leave next week. You can tell me about your classes and your job, but what I really want to know is have you met any Greek men!?

Sweat is pouring off of me and I'm starting to get a headache from the pounding bass and flashing lights. I let my hands wander over the hips of the girl I'm grinding behind, and she arches into me in response. The only problem is, I feel nothing. I'm not turned on, I'm not intrigued, I'm bored out of my fucking mind, and all I really want to do is go home and sit in front of the TV for a couple of hours.

"I'm taking a break, why don't you go dance with my friends," I shout into the girl's ear. She throws me a pouty face over her shoulder, then shakes her money maker off toward my buddies, the Agripas brothers, who are dancing a few feet away. Gabriel grabs her and pulls her into him, grinding on her like there's no tomorrow. He looks across the dance floor at me and gives me a chin lift in thanks for the enthusiastic prize I sent his way. I give him a thumbs-up and make my way back upstairs to the VIP table we've been camped at all night.

Even as crowded as it is, people part and move to the sides as I go across the room. It's a perk of being both tall and filthy rich. Everyone on the island knows who I am, and none of them want to get in my way. When I reach the table I throw myself down on one of the padded leather benches and lay my head back, staring at the ceiling. My cousin, Christos, slides a tumbler of something across the table to me.

"What's the matter with you? She looked plenty willing, why'd you leave her down there?"

I sigh. How can I explain the way I've been feeling lately? I certainly can't complain. Not about anything. I have the perfect life. More money than any one man could spend in two lifetimes, women of all sorts at my beck and call, good friends and family who worship me. I even have a pretty kickass job, all things considered. But I'm bored, and sometimes I even approach miserable. I'm tired of the parties, tired of the superficial hookups, and God forbid my father ever hear me say it, but I'm even kind of tired of the company.

"I don't know, man," I tell Christos. "Just not feeling it."

He looks at me thoughtfully. He's my cousin, but also my best friend. Really more like a brother. I've got four sisters, and a ton of cousins, but Christos is the one I'm closest to. We're only eight months apart in age, and his father is my dad's brother. We spent virtually every waking moment together as kids. We shared a tutor until we were old enough to go to boarding school in Athens and London. After that we went to Miami University and both played on the soccer team. Then we came back to Georgios and Dad made me CFO, and Christos the Manager of Accounts Receivable, one of the dozen departments that report directly to me.

"This is the third weekend in a row you don't want to party. What gives?"

This, right here, is why I don't complain. Christos and the family, they have these expectations of me. That I'll be the golden boy, happy, charming, surrounded by women, magnanimous to all. Georgios is a moderate-sized island, and for generations the Stephanos family has been the de facto kings here. We own a majority of the land, we run the island's principal employer, we have more money than the rest of the islanders combined. We have more money than much of the rest of the *world* combined actually.

And because of that, because we have that money, and that history, and because my father is like the patron of Georgios, I'm treated like its prince. But with that comes expectations. Expectations that I'll behave like a benign dictator, taking what's mine, giving scraps to the peasants, assuming my place in the family dynasty, and one day, when my father is no longer able to rule the kingdom, I'm destined to take over. My entire life has been mapped out for me since the day I was born, but I'm not sure it's the life I actually want.

And I can't tell Christos that. Because as much as my life's mapped out, so is his. He has the role of second son. He's my right-hand man, the guy whose job it is to keep me happy and safe. When we're not on Georgios I have bodyguards who travel with me, and Christos has been in charge of them since we were sixteen. Yeah, a sixteen-year-old boy was given the responsibility of keeping the heir to a multi-billion-dollar fortune safe. He had a whole slew of security specialists advising him of course, but my dad said Christos needed to settle in to his role as my *deftheri*, my closest advisor, the role he's expected to continue for life.

"Do you ever wish you had more choice?" I ask him, evading a precise answer to his question.

"What do you mean? More choice in girls?"

"No. God, get your brain out of your dick. More choice in life. Do you ever wonder what you'd do differently if you weren't a Stephanos? If you could choose where to live and what job to have."

He snorts as if it's the dumbest suggestion he's ever heard. "Hell no. Why would I? If I had a choice I'd choose to be a Stephanos and do exactly what I'm doing now." He waves an arm around the discotheque we're in, flashing lights, writhing bodies, booming bass. "It doesn't get much better than this, bro."

I give him a tight smile, knowing he'll never understand what I'm feeling. No one in my family will. They do things the same way, generation after generation, and I love them, but more and more lately

I'm not sure I love my life. Something is missing. I crave a challenge, a change of some sort.

Unbidden, an image of the girl I ran into at the docks yesterday pops into my head. Her blonde hair floating around her head in the breeze. Her sweet curves as she struggled with those bags that were as big as she was. I saw her long before she fell into my arms, in fact, I delayed the run I was going on because I saw her on the deck of the ferry.

There was something about her—she was so different than the girls I come into contact with every day. I see two basic types, the ones who are good Greek girls, raised to marry good Greek men, and the ones who are here at this club. Who will fuck me anytime I want them to, who are vapid and superficial. In a sense they're a modern version of the other type. Still spending their lives doing something to please the world around them. Marry me or fuck me, it all comes from the same place. Make the prince happy.

But I could tell that the blonde on the ship didn't fall into either of those categories—and not simply because she wasn't Greek—no, she was something different. You could see with one look that this girl knew exactly who she was, what she was doing, where she was going. Even her little outburst about the rules for disembarking was confident. Secretly I agree with her—there's no point in having the damn sign up if the rules it displays aren't going to be enforced, but I argued with her because it was a thing of beauty to watch her convictions. To see someone who was so secure in who they were and what they believed that they'd argue with a perfect stranger in a foreign country mere moments after landing.

And she left me thinking that I have no idea who *I* am or what *I* believe, because I've never had the chance to find out. Everything in my whole life has been handed to me on a platter. My interests, my occupation, my values, my very identity. Handed to me. No one ever asked, and that's what it comes down to. No matter how rich the prize, no one ever asked if I wanted it. I wish I could be as sure as Christos that this is where I belong, but lately I've been full of doubt, and that's fucking scary as hell, because I don't know that I'll ever have another choice.

**

Sunday morning means church in my family. Christos and I avoid it as much as possible—one, we're usually hungover from Saturday night, and two, Greek Orthodox church is a fucking nightmare of never-ending ceremonies and relatives pouring out of your ears—but at least once a month we have to show up, and today is that day.

"God my head hurts," Christos bitches as he adjusts his sunglasses while we hike up the walkway to the church. "I thought I'd never get Alexina out of my bed this morning. Her voice made my head pound like someone was hammering inside of it."

I stretch, exaggerating every movement and sound. "Yeaaah, those solid eight I got were sure restful. Whole bed to myself. Nice clean sheets. No screechy women."

"Dude. I got laid," Christos reminds me. "You had to jack off first thing this morning."

"Fuck off," I say right before I look up and see my mother standing on the church steps in front of me.

"Niko!" she snaps, giving me the look that's been guilting me into moderately good behavior for twenty-four years.

"Sorry, Ma. I'm sorry." I lean in and give her a kiss on each cheek. "Good morning. How are you?"

She smiles, placated by my chagrin, and then greets Christos too.

"I've got to go find my mom," he says. "She thought I'd never come to church again. I had to prove her wrong."

"And he gets sucked in by the reverse psychology yet again," I say to no one in particular.

"Let's go in," my mother says, hooking her hand through my elbow. "Daddy and the girls are seated already."

I'm about to follow her when I hear a husky voice behind me. "Niko. Fancy meeting you here."

I turn to find myself face to face with a very unhappy Juliet Papadous, my receptionist, and the woman I've been screwing for the last few weeks.

"Uh, Ma, I'll be there in a few minutes," I say, knowing that what's coming shouldn't take place inside a house of worship.

My mother gives me a tight smile and looks at Juliet like she's something that came off the sole of a shoe. Then she moves inside the building, and I gently walk Juliet a few feet away from the church doors, out of the main traffic path. I see all the older women in the congregation giving me the side-eye though, so I hope this doesn't get too ugly.

"Thanks for the phone calls," Juliet says without preamble.

I scratch the back of my head. I hate this crap. I don't run through women like Kleenex the way Christos does, but I also don't have girlfriends, so anyone who wants to chill with me should understand that. Juliet is hot, and I had fun with her, but it's not like I ever implied we were dating.

"Yeah, I've been tied up with things," I lie.

"Funny, because my friend Lisa said you were out clubbing with Christos last night."

"Look, Jules—"

"Don't you dare," she hisses. "Don't you dare give me some speech about how I should have known the score and you never promised me anything. Guys make promises in all kinds of ways, Niko. You didn't use words, but you've been sleeping in my bed and eating the food I cooked for you and sticking your hand up my skirt at work for the last three weeks. That implies certain things."

Yeah, I'm not seeing it, but whatever, she obviously has a different view.

"Look, I'm sorry if I misled you in any way. It wasn't my intention," I tell her. "The fact is, I'm just too busy for a real relationship right now. I like you, Jules, but I don't want a girlfriend at the moment."

Her eyes narrow and from the corner of my eye I see her arm draw back. No way is she going to fucking slap me on the church steps.

I grab her wrist before she can hit me, then I get close to her face, keeping my voice low, but putting every bit of future CEO I've got into it.

"Listen up, because I won't say this again. It was fun, but we're done. I have no problems with you, but if you have one with me that you can't get control of, then you know where the door is. I'll give you a glowing recommendation, but I won't put up with bullshit from you at work, or home, or in front of the goddamn church."

I think I may have just completely blown my chances at getting into heaven. I really need to control my language.

Juliet's eyes get wide, and I see her lip quiver ever so slightly. She's tough this one, but I can tell I've pierced the armor. I didn't want to do it, but it's better to nip this shit in the bud.

She wrenches her wrist from my hand and nods once. "Yes, sir, Mr. Stephanos," she whispers. Then she marches into the church, smoke practically rising from the earth she scorches when she goes.

It's going to be a long week at Stephanos Shipping.

CHAPTER THREE

Tess

ForeignXChange Group

Tess: Hey, Kellie. No. But I did meet a Greek boy.

I spend the next couple of days getting settled into my new place with Cass. It's a darling apartment on the third floor of a building that's probably a few hundred years old. We've got a living room with a tiny kitchen attached, a bathroom that we share with the old lady across the hall, and a bedroom that has space for two single beds, two dressers, and a wardrobe for hanging clothes.

Cass has made some space for my things in the wardrobe, but even with the meager amount of stuff I brought we realize we're going to have to find another place to hang things. I'm so glad Cass has the car because we end up driving to the hardware store and getting a wooden rod that we suspend from the ceiling next to the wardrobe. That then becomes my closet. It's all super boho, but I don't mind.

When Monday morning rolls around I'm unpacked, I know where the nearest grocery store is, and I'm relieved that my roommate is easy to get along with, plus has a boyfriend with his own place so I get plenty of "alone" time.

"Oh good, you're still here!" Cass cries out as she comes slamming into the apartment first thing in the morning. I'm drinking a cup of coffee and eating tiganites, which are Greek pancakes. She made them for me yesterday and there were extra which I'm now chowing down like this is my last meal.

I struggle to swallow before I answer her. "I don't have to be there until nine."

She tosses her purse on the table by the front door. "I wanted to be here to wish you good luck on your first day."

"Thank you," I say, once again thinking how lucky I was to get Cass for a roomie. "I'm glad I chose to start the internship a week earlier than school. I'm nervous enough about this as it is, I can't imagine if I had to start classes today too."

She sits down at the kitchen table and snatches a piece of food off of my plate. "I cooked these for Anton this morning," she says, referring to her boyfriend whose place she slept at last night. "He ate the entire batch in five minutes."

I shake my head and roll my eyes. "Boys," I say. "When my brother, Nate, was in college he used to come home for breaks and I'd find him in the kitchen with a box of cereal, a half gallon of milk and a mixing bowl. He'd pour the entire box in, the whole carton of milk, and then eat it all with a giant serving spoon. Yet, he sill weighed less than most of the girls on the soccer team."

"If I ate like that—" Cass grabs another piece of my tiganites and I push the plate toward her. I'm too nervous to eat much anyway. "—I'd *be* the soccer team."

Talking about my brother reminds me of the email I read from him when I woke up this morning. Nate's an FBI agent. Not the kind who goes around in dark cars with RayBans on, but one who sits in front of a computer and watches hackers and pedophiles as they try to use the Internet to further their criminal enterprises. He does with technology what I hope to do with numbers. Nate must have seen something about Stephanos Shipping at work because he wrote me a cautionary email:

To: TessR@chiu.edu
From: NR280@fbi.gov

Hey Mess (yeah, he turned Tess into Mess early on in my life),

Hope everything's good in Greece. Mom said you got there okay. I'm glad you have a roommate, you can't be too careful alone in a foreign country (and yes, he's in law enforcement and I'm his baby sister, hence the overprotectiveness). *Mom also told me about the*

*company they've got you interning at. I'm not so sure
your school's done their research. If it were up to me
you'd skip the internship and stick to the classes while
you're there.*

Now here's where the problem comes in. Nate can't
talk about things he knows from work, it's all classified
information. But sometimes he finds out things that
relate to friends or family—a hotel that's broken
gambling regulations, a pediatrician who's being
investigated for improprieties—things that he
desperately wants to warn people about and can't. So,
he uses as many generalizations as possible. He warns
people without actually warning them. It's tricky.

*If you do keep that internship, make sure you tell me
how it's going. Send me an email at work if there's
anything at all that doesn't seem right. You know what
I'm saying, Mess, right?*

*Also, don't go anywhere with any Greek guys. I
mean it.*

You suck,
Nate.

As I recall his email, it makes me even more
nervous about my first day of work. It's probably
something stupid like he's found out Stephanos didn't
pay a tariff when they entered US waters, I really
shouldn't give it a second thought. I try to shake off the
nervousness his email left me with. I remind myself that
Nate is way overprotective. I'm not going to skip
meeting Greek guys because of his warnings, why
would I quit my totally awesome internship because of
them?

"Earth to Tess," Cass says with a smirk on her face. "Thinking about your new boss?"

I snort. "No. God. I probably won't even see him. I'm sure he only deals with the senior accountants, not college interns."

"Well, you know there are a lot of stories about interns and their bosses—Monica Lewinsky, Cecilia West…"

"Shut up!" I smack her on the arm. I feel my cheeks heat, and somewhere in the back of my mind is a flash of an image—me, Niko Stephanos, a desk, papers scattering, skin sliding, clothes rumpling. I take a deep breath, squashing the desire to fan myself. Change the subject. Quick.

"What's going to happen with you and Anton when you go back to Chicago to finish school?" I ask the first thing that pops into my head.

Cass grins, an all too knowing look on her face. "We'll be apart some in the spring, but he's going to come see me once, and I'm going to come back to see him once. Then in May I'll be returning to start a job at my aunt's shop. I worked there all summer too, but I won't be now that school is starting back up."

"You have family here?" I ask, suddenly understanding why she speaks so much Greek and seems so comfortable with the whole place.

"Yeah, my mom is Greek and her family still lives here. She met my dad when he was stationed in Athens for a year. He married her, took her back to the States, and the rest is family history."

I stand and take the empty dishes to the sink where I rinse them and load them into the miniature dishwasher.

"That's really cool."

"What's even cooler is that my aunt loaned me that car. You want a ride to work?"

I know eventually I'm going to have to learn the bus system, but for now, as nervous as I am? I can be independent later. After I've faced down my first day at an office where they don't speak English and my new boss is a cocky billionaire.

"Yes, please." I grin at Cass.

"Good, but before we go, put on some higher heels. You need to show Niko Stephanos that he can't mess with you, and he'll never buy it if you look like a Polly Pocket doll."

Being short sucks.

**

The receptionist in the accounting department at Stephanos Shipping speaks perfect English. She's also five foot nine, voluptuous and perfectly put together in that way only European women can be. Her skirt and blouse are relatively conservative, but display her figure to perfection. She's statuesque with long, dark, glossy hair and perfect make-up.

"I'm Juliet," she says as she rises from her desk to shake my hand.

"It's nice to meet you. And I'm so glad you speak English. I want to learn as much Greek as I can while I'm here, but it's not really a language you can take a lot of courses in at American Universities. So I don't know any yet, but the foreign exchange office at my school said there would be someone who spoke English for me here at the internship." I stop, having run out of breath, and yeah, I'm really nervous and I need to shut up.

Juliet looks at me with an indulgent expression. "Stephanos is an *international* corporation," she tells me smugly. "*All* of our employees speak multiple languages. I imagine *you* will be the only one who doesn't."

Oh. Okay. Well, that was embarrassing. I swallow and try to stand up straighter. Maybe even these heels aren't tall enough to garner me respect.

"If you'll come this way there's a staff meeting every Monday morning. We can get you set up at your desk afterwards."

I follow tall and crabby through a maze of hallways and cubicles until we get to a back conference room that holds about a dozen people at a table and another dozen in chairs around the perimeter of the room. The Stephanos shipping offices are right next to the dock where I disembarked two days ago. Several squat, white buildings line the corridor along the docks, and across the street enormous ships with "Stephanos Shipping" stamped on their hulls lurk, taking up all the good ocean frontage on this side of the island.

When we arrive at the conference room Juliet gestures for me to take one of the leftover chairs along the wall while she gracefully slides into a seat next to the head of the table. Everyone is murmuring amongst themselves and I take a look around. No one seems to notice me. Most of the people are older, but there are two women and one guy who look closer to my age. The guy is good looking in that typical Greek way— olive skin, dark hair, metrosexual European clothes. He reminds me a little of Niko, but without the raw sexuality that Niko has, that magnetism that makes you feel lightheaded and overheated.

I find myself wondering how old Niko is? Is it hard for him to be the boss of people who are so much older than he is? I also wonder what being the boss means here. Does he actually do stuff like come to staff meetings, or do his minions handle all that for him?

The door to the room swings open and a deep voice chuckles before saying, "Okay Brian, we'll get those numbers out to you today. This is going to be a great project. Looking forward to it." My eyes snap up right as Niko reaches the conference table and ends the call. Everyone in the room shifts a touch in their seats like they're all drawn to the magnetic presence at the front. I blink, sort of mesmerized myself. He's the sun and I'm only a lowly planet.

His thick hair is gelled into submission, and his eyes are made even bluer by the contrast with that dark, shiny mass of waves. He's wearing black narrow cut slacks with a white dress shirt but no jacket or tie, and he's already rolled up the sleeves. When my gaze reaches his hands I'm reminded of what it felt like to have them touch me when he caught me off the end of the gangplank. Heat flows through me like a wave of liquid lava. His fingers are long and perfectly manicured, but not effeminate. No, his hands definitely look strong and capable. Of many things. I work to catch a breath.

"Excuse me for being late," he says, shuffling the stack of papers sitting in front of his chair before he looks up to greet the room. His eyes fall on me immediately, and he pauses for a split second. Maybe no one else notices, but I do. The pause is followed by a slow, cocky twist of his lips as he shifts his eyes from me to the rest of the room.

"I hope you all had a good weekend?" he prompts. Everyone answers in the affirmative, and that knowing little smile on his face grows bigger before he looks back to me.

"We seem to have someone new here today. Would you like to introduce yourself?" he asks, gesturing my direction.

My throat is dry and tight, and I'm having a difficult time catching my breath. The spark in his eyes says he's enjoying putting me on the spot. Bastard. I take a breath, and prepare for battle.

"My name is Tess Richardson," I say, voice a little quivery. I hate when that happens. I take a deep breath and feel better when I sound stronger. "I'm a new intern majoring in forensic accounting at Chicago University, and I'll be continuing my coursework at the American University here. I'm afraid that I don't speak Greek—yet—but I want to learn, so feel free to teach me as much as you can. About Greek *and* accounting."

When I'm done I look around. For the most part people look friendly enough. The good-looking guy I noticed earlier is grinning at me like I'm the most interesting thing to come to Stephanos Shipping in years. I give him a little smile back and he winks. My eyes land on Niko next. He scowls at the other guy, then turns to me.

"Welcome to Stephanos," he says, his face giving away nothing. "I'll let everyone introduce themselves as we run through the meeting, but if you'll stay afterwards, you and I can have a chat."

Then he drops the bomb.

"You'll be working directly for me."

**

This. Can not. Be happening. The meeting has ended although I couldn't for the life of me tell you what it was about. I know people told me their names, I know each division gave some sort of report, beyond that it was all a low grade buzzing around me as I silently went batshit crazy inside my head. Working directly for him? For the billionaire brat who doesn't think rules apply? For the most gorgeous and irritating man I've ever met? I am so screwed.

First of all, he's going to make me work in a dark pit somewhere to punish me for my insolence. Then I'm going to have to watch that sexy smirk every single day while he undoubtedly gives me the worst assignments in the whole company. And to top it all off, every woman in the office hates my guts now. Tall and perfect Juliet spent the rest of the meeting shooting daggers at me with her professionally made-up smoky eyes. She doesn't realize that he isn't doing this to hit on me, he's doing it to torture me.

As people file out of the room they murmur "goodbye" and "welcome to the team" things at me. A couple of the women give me the once over, sneering at my obviously American, obviously college girl cheap clothes. They're all so sophisticated and European. My plain black cotton skirt and white button up blouse make me look like a waitress. Thank God Cass made me put on the heels. They're the only thing saving me from total fashion humiliation.

And then we're alone. Niko Stephanos and me. I stand up as straight as I can and take a step toward the conference table where he's looking down at his phone screen.

"It's nice to meet you formally," I say as business-like as possible, extending my hand to shake his.

He looks up at me and a wry smile spreads across his incredibly handsome features. He leans a hip against the table and crosses his arms. "Yes. Isn't it though?"

My heart skips a beat. It's because I'm scared of what he's going to do to me, not because his biceps are straining against that finely woven shirt, his throat like a golden column rising from the snowy whiteness.

I take my hand back since he's obviously not going to shake it, and stand in awkward silence, not sure what to say. I can tell he's enjoying it. Then, when I think I might scream or cry merely to break the discomfort, he drawls, "We have some *rules* here at Stephanos—"

I grimace, waiting for the hammer to fall.

"So I think you'd better start learning them." He walks over to a bookshelf in the corner and grabs a five-inch thick binder. The damn thing easily weighs as much as I do. He ambles back toward me and holds it out, one eyebrow raised.

"You're kidding, right?" Shit. There went my pretense of acting professionally with this guy.

"I thought you liked rules?" he says.

"I think they're important for society to function properly."

"And I think they're important for my company to function properly," he responds, still holding out the binder.

I look down at the cover. It's in Greek. "I can't read that, you know. It's in Greek." I can't help the smile of triumph that I struggle to keep smothered.

He drops the tome on the table in front of me. "English is on the backside of each page," he quips.

Dammit. My heart sinks.

"Read the first three chapters on our personnel policies and my secretary will come get you in a bit to show you your office."

Oh. Only the first three chapters? I look up and see his cocky grin. He did that on purpose. He's totally screwing with me.

My eyes narrow and I grit my teeth. A small growl works its way up my throat, but is silenced before it can escape because he leans in right next to my ear and whispers, his breath hot, his words silky, "This is going to be fun." Then he strolls past me, a single finger grazing the skin on my arm as he passes, leaving behind a trail of fire. Seriously. I'm. On. Fire.

When the door to the room shuts behind him I'm still standing there, trying to remember how to breathe.

**

"He said what?!" Cass hollers at me from the kitchen as I stand in the middle of our living room.

"You heard me," I answer, throwing myself on the couch and burying my head in a pillow.

"What does that mean?" she asks, her voice closer. I lift my head and she's there, a chunk of baklava on a plate in her hand. She sets it down on the coffee table, hands me one of the forks, and flops next to me. We

31

both dig into the honey-drenched pastry, and I can't help but moan in delight, talking with a full mouth.

"Most likely that he's going to enjoy tormenting me because I was so surly to him at the docks the other day."

Cass grunts and mutters, "Yeah, right."

"What?"

"I think he's talking about fun, like fun in your pants kind of fun."

I choke and give myself a coughing fit. What the hell?

"Fun in your pants? What are we, twelve?"

"I'm just sayin', you didn't see the way he was looking at you at the docks—like he wanted to have you for dinner. I don't think he's intending to torment you, at least not the way you're supposing."

A shiver runs through me at the mere thought of being tormented by Niko Stephanos that way. Yum.

"As delicious as that could be, it would never happen. We're total opposites and I can tell he hates me. It's going to suck working for someone who wants to see me miserable all year."

Cass snorts. "You keep telling yourself that. And call me when you wake up in his bed one of these days."

I roll my eyes. "He's gorgeous, I grant you that, but he's really not my type."

Cass stands and picks up the empty baklava plate. "Tess. Niko Stephanos is every woman's type."

I stare out the window and sigh as she cleans up the kitchen. I'm afraid that she might be right, and I might be in really big trouble.

CHAPTER FOUR

Niko

ForeignXChange Group

Darla: OMG, I'm in Spain and it is muy excelente! Fiestas todo el tiempo I say. Oops, gotta go—Felipe is waiting!

I wake up Wednesday morning before work and come to a realization—I want Tess Richardson. Plain and simple. I couldn't get her out of my head all weekend, and when I walked into the office Monday and saw her sitting there in my conference room, I knew that once again the universe had handed something to me on a platter. But this time I won't complain. In fact, this time, I'll give thanks to whoever set this whole thing up—the gods of internships or whatever—because Tess is the most interesting thing to enter my world in a very long time.

She's like this tiny ball of conviction and determination. The way she stood in that staff meeting, nervous as I could see she was, and faced down a roomful of older people, her eyes flashing and her voice becoming stronger with each word she spoke. There she was, two days in a foreign country, admitting she doesn't speak a word of the native language, but ready to work her hardest and learn whatever it is she needs to in order to succeed. I've never met anyone quite like her.

And God she's fun to tease. The look on her face when I tried to hand her that giant binder of crap that no one in our office has ever read, was priceless. I could have told her everything I needed her to know about our personnel policies in about two minutes, but since she loves rules so much I figured why not let her read the damn policies for herself? *I* don't even know what's in those policies. I think the only reason we have them is because my cousin Mira went to the London School of Economics and learned all about human resources, so to be supportive my dad let her write us a bunch of personnel regulations. All Tess really needs to know is that payday happens every other Friday, we open the doors at nine a.m., and lunch is from noon to two. That pretty much sums up the rules in my office.

The good news in all of this is that there are no rules in my world that say I can't go after Tess—intern or not. Yeah, I've spent enough time in the US and UK to know that it's frowned upon there. Person in a position of power and everything, but none of that has anything to do with what happens outside the office, and I'm thinking there are all sorts of things that could happen.

As I finish off my cup of coffee and hand it to my housekeeper, I grab my car keys off of the table in the front hallway of the villa I share with Christos. My mother will never understand why I don't live with the family since I'm not married, but my dad gets that, at my age, a guy wants his own space. Eventually I'll have to get married and have kids to carry on the family business, but no one's rushing me, so for now, I date— a lot—and Christos and I live in the villa my dad bought for us, complete with housekeeper, gardener, and a chauffeur that I refuse to use. Driving my vintage Aston Martin is something I'm not willing to give up.

As I head outside to hop in the car, the sun is shining, the sky is clear, and I'm smiling because I've got a new prize to pursue, at a moment when I thought I'd already won every prize there was to have.

**

My good mood is shattered when I walk into the office and am greeted by a very pissed off Juliet.

"Mr. Stephanos," she hisses as I walk past her desk on the way to my office.

"Good morning," I mutter, hoping like hell that she'll leave it at this and let me get on with my day.

"May I have a word?" she asks, flashing me a seriously psychotic smile.

I sigh and turn back to her. "What is it Jules?"

"I thought you should know that I have an appointment with your father."

I feel my eye twitch. "Okay. Is there some reason why you wouldn't go to your immediate supervisor—me—first?"

"I did go to you. You'll recall our discussion at church last weekend?"

I nod, every muscle in my body growing tenser.

"In said discussion you threatened my job, Mr. Stephanos. Because I dared to ask why you had suddenly ended our personal relationship with no warning. I shouldn't be punished because I questioned your morals."

My morals? Does she remember some of the things we did in her bed? And they weren't all my ideas either. Juliet's got some pretty damn questionable morals if you ask me.

"Look, Jules, do what you got to do. But you're wasting your time and my dad's. He doesn't give a shit about your hurt feelings. All I said was that I don't want a bunch of crap here at the office—crap like this. Just let it go and we can get back to normal. You answer the phones, I sign the paychecks. It's easy."

I see her fist clenched at her side, but I don't stick around for more drama. I stride full tilt to my office and shut the door after I get inside. I hate this shit. It makes me want to go out on the water and not come back in again. But then again, if I didn't come in to work I wouldn't get to see Tess, and that's something I'm not willing to give up. I can only hope that she wasn't around to see Juliet's latest display. It's going to be hard enough convincing her to go out with me. The last thing I need is for her to think I drag a slew of baggage along behind me.

**

Fun. It is fun to walk through the office and see Tess sitting at her little desk in the cubicle right outside my door.

But today my fun is derailed as I see that Tess isn't at her desk. I saunter over, taking a cursory look at the few belongings she's placed there in the two days since she started working for me. A cup of coffee, an iPhone charger, and a bus schedule, which is in Greek, so she'll never be able to understand it.

"She's in but I sent her down to the mailroom," my secretary, Annais, says. "Do you need something?"

Annais is a few years older than me and one of my second cousins. Probably half of the staff here in Georgios is related to me either by blood or marriage. The good thing is, because she's my cousin and she's married, I don't have to worry about her hating on me like Juliet.

"Just tell Tess to come see me when she gets back," I say to Annais before moving on to my office. Annais gives me a look that says she doesn't approve of me meeting with Tess. That look makes me tired. But not too tired to meet with Tess.

I get to my desk and start the tedious exercise of going through my email inbox. There are four sections in the company—finance, operations, administration, and marketing. My dad's plan is to have me lead each section for two to three years, until I've rotated through all of them. Then he'll make me CEO while he takes on the presidency of the board. Right now my Uncle Tomas, Christos's father, is president of the board, and my dad is CEO. Dad says he wants to retire in ten years. I'll believe it when I see it. And ultimately, what really matters is that my dad has a very large controlling interest in the company, so until he dies and leaves that to me, he's the boss no matter what title he takes on.

I wanted to spend some time aggravating Tess the last two days, but I've been in and out of meetings my dad set up for me nearly the entire time she's been working here. I've had to sit around in conference rooms and restaurants and my parents' villa listening to some of our biggest clients discuss what they need from Stephanos over the next year. It's an annual thing my dad does—asks the customers to help us prioritize.

In January we'll come out with a report that details our next year's goals and includes some of the things our VIP clients mentioned. It's good business, and I appreciate that my dad is a savvy businessman to include his customers like he does, but I wasn't in the mood for it this year, and watching a bunch of middle-aged men with oversized guts swig my dad's wine and devour his food for two straight days hasn't done much to increase my general enthusiasm for my job.

But today they've all gone home and I can turn my attentions to something far more interesting—Tess Richardson.

A throat clearing has my eyes lifting from the computer screen. Speak of the devil.

"Annais said you wanted to see me?"

She's wearing a pair of dark skinny jeans with a blue and white striped top and a denim blazer. On her feet are some of the highest heels I've ever seen—navy blue with a little cutout at the tips of the toes. Her tiny toenails are bright red, and I can't help the smile that crawls across my face.

"Yes. Come in," I say as I walk out from behind my desk and gesture to the seating area at the other end of my office. I shut the door after she comes in and I see her stiffen at the noise of the latch closing. Good, she can think of me as the big bad wolf, I'll huff, and I'll puff, and if I'm lucky she'll blow—well, maybe I'd better stop that thought right there.

She sits on the sofa and I choose the armchair across from her. She's so prim and proper it kills me. And it makes me want to muss her up, in the best possible way.

"I'm sorry I haven't been able to check in with you sooner," I tell her. "It's been a busy few days. I wanted to see how everything's going though. You're learning your way around?"

She nods enthusiastically. "Yes, Annais has been very helpful."

"And the work you're doing is okay? Do you feel like you're learning something?"

"Definitely. The first account you assigned me to— the Yarros produce account—it's big enough to be a challenge, but not overwhelming. And Annais said one of the senior accountants will double-check all of my work."

I nod. She's so earnest and serious. I admire it, and also think it's cute.

"And what do you think of Georgios so far?"

A little line appears between her eyebrows. I think she's not as sure about this line of questioning.

"It's nice, although I haven't seen a lot of it. But my roommate showed me our neighborhood and Christos has offered to take me to lunch today so we can walk around the central part of town while we're out. He's been really generous with his time."

Christos. That motherfucker. I should have known. He made a big deal out of telling me how hot he thought she was after work on Monday, but I've been so busy I haven't had a chance to tell him to keep his dirty paws off of my prize. I saw her first.

I grind my teeth as I plaster on a smile. "Well, my cousin is nothing if not generous. And it works out perfectly because I've got lunch free today so I can go with you. We'll take you to our favorite restaurant here on the waterfront and then show you downtown."

Her eyes grow big. "Uh, you're going to come with us?" she squeaks. "You can't really have time for that...right?"

Huh. Maybe she wishes she could go to lunch with Christos alone? Not a chance, princess.

"I've got plenty of time, and I owe it to my favorite new employee." I grin, she balks.

"Listen," she says, looking down at her hands folded so carefully in her lap. "We sort of got off to a bad start at the docks, and I've never apologized. I mean, if I'd known you were going to be my boss I would have never talked to you that way—obviously."

I raise one eyebrow and look at her.

She takes a deep breath. "So I hope there are no hard feelings?"

Some things feel hard when I'm sitting here like this with Tess, but that's not what she's referring to I know.

I lean forward, looking her in the eyes. I see her swallow, and watch the muscles in her slender neck work, undulating like tiny waves in the ocean.

"There aren't any hard feelings, princess. I get it, you're a good girl, you like to follow the rules."

She nods, smiling like she's so relieved that I finally understand.

"But see, I'm not a good boy. I don't follow anyone's rules—they follow mine." I hear her sharp intake of breath and it sends a rush of satisfaction coursing through me.

"I've decided it's my duty, as the first person you encountered when you set foot on Georgios, to loosen you up. Help bust you out of your good girl mold." Her eyes grow bigger yet, and her lips part. I'm entranced by them. Like two perfectly round little cherries just begging to be sucked.

"I'm going to teach you how to break the rules, princess."

Her voice is breathy when she answers me. "What if I don't want to learn?"

"Oh, you will," I tell her darkly. "Nothing goes with Greece's sun and sand like a little sin."

CHAPTER FIVE

Tess

ForeignXChange Group

Tess: So, Darla, wow. Be careful you don't fiesta with any illegal substances, they kick you out of the program for that.

I'm in the bathroom at work freaking out. "Yes, I'm serious!" I whisper shout to Cass as I sit on the lid of a toilet in one of the stalls.

"What rules exactly is he talking about?" she asks, being very literal about the whole thing.

"How should I know? But he talked about sun and sin and he was all leery and stuff." My heart is racing and I have a chunk of my own hair wrapped around my hand as I babble at Cass hysterically.

"What the hell does leery mean?"

I try to take a full breath and calm down. "You know...alpha and pervy and stuff."

Cass cracks up, and I have to listen to her laughing her ass off for at least half a minute. When she finally catches her breath and calms down she says, "Alpha and pervy? Have you been reading Fifty Shades or something? What does that even mean? Did he want to tie you up? Or maybe he suggested anal? Which actually, wouldn't surprise me. He's so rich, he probably is like a Christian Grey—dirty and bored."

"Oh my God." I roll my eyes. "He did not say anything like that, he just made every comment seem like it had a second meaning. The way 'sun and sand and sin' rolled off his tongue—" a small shiver rolls down my spine, "—it was like he was wrapping his mouth around a really sexy ice cream cone."

"Wow. I think I just came a little," she deadpans.

"You know what I mean!" I hiss.

She must be eating something because I hear her chomping as she talks around what sounds like a mouthful of cotton.

"Yes, of course I know what you mean. I'm giving you a hard time, but really, are you that surprised? I told you he was giving you the look at the docks last weekend. He has the hots for you. I say go for it."

I twist sideways and lean my head back against the metal wall of the stall. It's tempting. Really tempting. He's hot, and overbearing, and all those things they say women aren't supposed to find attractive, but we all secretly do. He's also spoiled, entitled and most of all— my boss. We have nothing in common. I'm a middle-class girl from Illinois. He's a billionaire from Greece. I can't even conceive of the things he's probably seen and done. And he obviously doesn't understand the world I'm from, a world where following the rules is what insures you'll succeed.

"I can't," I tell Cass, hearing the despondency in my own voice. "As much as I'd like to, I can't risk it. If I lost this internship I couldn't pay for living here this year, and I've already missed the start of the semester back home. It would set back my whole graduation if I had to stay in school an extra term." I sigh. "He's got all the power here, and if he decides after some one-night stand that he doesn't want me working here anymore, I'm screwed."

"Ah but what a screwing it would be," Cass sighs. "I understand what you're saying though. You're being the grown up, and I admire you for sticking to your principles."

"Remind me of that when I'm sitting home alone this weekend with nothing but ice cream and the pleasurette." I stand and smooth out my top. I've been in here for five minutes freaking out. Normally you're allowed one fifteen-minute break for every four hours you work, so I don't want to use up my whole break time before I've even been in the office for three hours.

Cass gasps. "Oooh, do you have one of those new small ones?" she asks.

I roll my eyes. I should have known she'd be an expert on vibrators.

"No. I was joking actually. I don't own one. Of any kind. Small or otherwise," I clarify.

"Oh." I can hear her disappointment and I have to smile.

"What do you care anyway? You've got Anton."

"True. But it's going to be a long spring in Chicago without him. I wanted recommendations."

"I'll do some research online for you this weekend—while I'm sitting at home eating ice cream."

"Oh good!" I can picture her jumping up and down and clapping her hands. "You going to be okay now?" she asks.

"Yes. Thank you so much for listening to me freak out. I realize you just met me a few days ago. I promise I'm not normally so unstable."

She laughs. "It's okay. I get it. You don't know anyone else here and honestly, I like it. My old roommate left at the beginning of the summer, so I haven't had anyone around like this for a while now. It's really great having you here."

Aww. Now I feel lots better. "Thank you, Cass. I'm so glad we're roomies too."

I hang up and exit the stall, expecting to find myself alone, but there, leaning against a sink is Juliet, grumpiest receptionist on the planet.

"Uh, hi," I manage to squeak out, my heart racing that she's heard my conversation.

"Yes, I did hear you," she says, raising one eyebrow before she turns to the mirror and pulls out a tube of dark red lipstick.

I swallow, and give her a pleading look. I have no idea what to say in a circumstance like this.

"I'll go out on a limb here and assume you were referring to our very own young executive of the year, Niko Stephanos?"

"Um, look, I shouldn't have been having that conversation at work. I'm sorry. Can you please pretend like you never heard it?"

Her face softens a touch, and she gives one more dab to the lipstick before turning to face me again.

"A word of warning," she says. "All of your fears about job security when it comes to sleeping with the boss are warranted. I say this from experience. Things can get nasty when the prince is inconvenienced."

"Oh. Gosh. I'm sorry. For whatever you've been through. And I have no interest in sleeping with any of my bosses. So, no worries there."

She purses her lips and nods slowly. "Mmhm. Well, he can be pretty convincing when he wants to be, so as I said, heed the warning. And good luck."

She grabs her purse off the shelf and struts out of the room, never giving a look back. I slump against the counter and sigh. This is why there are rules, people. This is why there are rules.

CHAPTER SIX

Niko

ForeignXChange Group

Trish: Does wine count as an illegal substance? I think I drank an entire bottle last night at the Rue du something or other. Now I have to le puke. Please excusez-moi.

When Tess leaves my office I call Christos. "Come down here. We need to talk."

He slouches in, a cup of coffee in one hand and his phone in the other. He's constantly on that damn thing texting with whatever girl he can corral to arrange parties and meet-ups at the nightclubs for us. He claims he's doing his job keeping me entertained, but the fact is he's a player and loves hooking up with a different woman every night.

"What's up?" he says, flopping into one of the chairs facing my desk.

"You have lunch plans?" I ask, not looking up from the stack of papers I'm sorting through. I've got a million and one invoices to sign off on and some days it feels like I'll never be caught up.

"Actually, I do." I look up and he's grinning. It pisses me off even though I'm not sure why. "But if you need me for something I can cancel."

"Lunch plans with Tess?"

"Yeah…If you knew that, why'd you ask?" He's looking at me like a puppy that doesn't understand the command.

"I'm going too," I tell him. Then I sit and wait to see what he'll do. We've never clashed over a girl before. I've never cared enough to bother. One of us picks, then the other one takes whoever else is there. It's no big deal. But like I said, Tess is different than the girls we're usually with, and for some reason I don't want to give that opportunity up.

"Oh-kay," he draws out the word. "I was going to take her on a little walking tour down in this part of town. You can come along I guess. Might put a crimp in my game though, bro."

I lean back in my chair. This is when it's good to be the prince. "Yeah, about that. I want you to take your game elsewhere. I'm calling dibs on Tess."

He stares at me for a moment, and I think I see a flash of something in his eyes, but then he's back to his relaxed, cheerful self in mere seconds. "Sure thing, I didn't know you were interested. What brought this on? She's not really your type."

I snort. Tess is every guy's type. Blonde, curvy, earnest, smart. I guess if you only want a screw with big tits and no strings maybe she wouldn't be your go-to girl, but if you're looking for the total package? I'd say she's it.

"Well, she is for now," I tell him. "So where we going for lunch?" I grin and he shakes his head.

"Whatever. Your game, you choose."

"Andropov's?" I ask.

"Cool. I'll see you both at noon."

After he leaves I lean back and swivel to look out the window. I've got a view out over the water, and to my right is the hull of one of our giant tankers we use to ship large containers of hazardous liquids, mostly gasoline. Georgios's a tiny port, we have virtually nothing shipping out and only a relatively small amount of things shipping in, but my dad likes to keep some of the older ships docked here so that the people of Georgios know that he remembers it all started here. This is the heart and home of Stephanos Shipping.

Today the tanker is being loaded, which is odd, since we produce nothing here on the island that would need to be shipped on a tanker. But I see a couple of guys with large wooden crates on dollies that they're running up the gangplank onto the deck of the ship. I watch for a few more moments, as another pair loads an identical set of crates. I write down the number painted on the ship's hull with a note to myself to check up on it later. It's probably some sort of supplies they needed for the crew, but it doesn't hurt to check. The phone rings, I shove the piece of paper into my top desk drawer, and answer the call. The work never waits.

**

I've nearly forgotten Juliet's threats from a couple of days ago, but when my dad's secretary calls me to come up to his office I'm reminded that she's probably gone and complained and now I'm going to get chewed out.

"What's going on Pop?" I ask as I walk into his large office suite that sits almost directly above mine.

He stands and comes around his desk, grabbing my shoulders and planting a kiss on each cheek. "You didn't stay for dinner after church on Sunday."

"Yeah, Christos and I had a long night Saturday. We needed a little more rest and a little less of screaming relatives."

My dad shakes his head, but chuckles too as he returns to his chair and gestures at me to take a seat in front of his desk.

"You boys enjoy your freedom now. In a few years your mother will expect some grandchildren and you'll need to find a nice girl to settle down with."

My father is shorter than me, but I remember when I was a kid, he seemed like a giant. He's a barrel-chested man, with the same thick, dark hair and light blue eyes as me. I got my mother's somewhat longer and slimmer physique. My dad is a brute, from a long line of fishermen. No matter how expensive the suit, he never looks like one of those metrosexual guys in GQ.

He joined the Greek Navy right out of school. After his service was up he took over the family business and spent a few years building up the connections in the US and the UK. His English is adequate, but not as fluent as Christos and I, who grew up speaking it in boarding school and college.

"Pop, I know you didn't call me here to pressure me into getting married."

He looks at me and leans back in his chair, CEO style.

"Your receptionist was in my office a few days ago."

I sigh. God, why me? "Yeah, she might have mentioned she was going to do that."

His brow furrows, bringing his salt and pepper hairline further down his forehead. He looks more like a grumpy bear than usual now.

"You know I let you boys be boys. I understand there are lots of pretty women around, lots of chances for you to enjoy being young."

I nod, knowing what's coming next.

"Which is why you don't need to include the staff in your office as part of the pool. Go swim somewhere else, Niko."

I slouch in the chair, lying my head on the back and rolling my eyes to the ceiling. "Okay, I get it Pop. The woman is nuts, you know, it's not like I'm slowly making my way through the office defiling every female we employ."

He chuckles. "She was, what's the expression? Wound tight?"

"Yes," I answer. "That."

"And I've assured her that her job is safe, and you won't do anything mean to her, so be nice—not too nice—and my guess is it'll pass."

I sit back up straight. "Okay, I got it."

"But, no more dating your staff, right?"

I think about Tess, her beautiful smile and sexy curves flash through my head, causing a tingle to work its way up through my gut.

"Right. I hear you," I answer, not making any promises I can't or won't keep.

"Good boy," Dad says, standing and walking with me to the door. "I'll tell your mother you're coming to dinner after church next Sunday. You and Christos take it easy on the parties Saturday night, yes?"

"Yeah, Pop. We will."

He grabs my head with one hand and looks me in the eyes. "You're my heart, you know that, right?"

I smile. "Yes, I do."

He kisses me on both cheeks again. "Good. Go make me proud."

"I'll do my best, old man."

CHAPTER SEVEN

Tess

ForeignXChange Group

Tess: Remember that Greek boy I mentioned? He's my new boss. How do you say 'just fuck me now' in Greek?

At lunchtime Christos shows up at my desk first. He's a nice guy, a fun guy. Definitely not someone you'd ever consider as boyfriend material or anything, but the kind of guy you can flirt with and hang out with and not have to worry he'd take you too seriously or have expectations. Sort of the opposite of his cousin.

He leans a hip against my desk and crosses his arms.

"What are you doing?" he asks, a grin on his face.

I smile up at him. "I'm waiting for some guy in my office to come get me for lunch. I was about to gnaw my own arm off."

"So sorry," he says with his charming mixture of UK, US, and Greek accent. He and Niko both have that. A hint of Greek and British thrown in with their mostly American English. It's mysterious and only adds to their hotness of course.

I can't help but glance at the door to Niko's office. Maybe he didn't tell Christos and we can slip out of here before he realizes.

I put on my most upbeat smile. "Let's go before I faint."

Christos suddenly looks a bit uncomfortable as he pushes away from my desk and stands straight. His eyes dart to the door of Niko's office. "We uh, need to get—"

Right then, the door opens and out strides Niko, his jacket gone, his shirtsleeves rolled up, tan forearms flexing as he lifts his designer sunglasses to his face. He stops at my desk, looking first at Christos, whose lips press into a thin line momentarily, then at me, before he slides the sunglasses into place.

"Everyone ready?" he asks.

I swallow and look at Christos who shrugs in response, as if to say, *what can I do?* Right. What *can* he do?

"Yeah man," he tells Niko. "Let's go."

We walk along the waterfront for a few blocks until we reach a tiny hole-in-the-wall restaurant with a seating area literally on top of the water. If you lean too far one direction in your chair, you'll end up in the harbor.

Christos is quiet most of the way, while Niko spends the whole time pointing things out to me—different buildings, their history and role in the community. I have to say I'm impressed with his knowledge of the island. I don't know half as much about the town I grew up in.

When we get to the restaurant, Niko politely asks if there's any type of food item I'm allergic to or can't stand. I tell him no—I really like most food, probably a little too much if my ass is any indication. He says he'll choose for me since the menu's in Greek, and I'm fine with that. He and Christos get me settled at a table on the edge of the patio and go on up to the counter to put in our order.

I look out at the small harbor, the sun glinting off of the azure blue waters. I can hear the voices and noises of the town behind me, but the water has a sort of unique quiet to it—waves lapping at the concrete pilings of the building I'm in, breeze puffing softly across the surface. Even the sounds of the gulls looping up and down over the ocean are muted.

"It's beautiful, isn't it?" Niko asks as he sits down across from me.

I nod my head. "It is. Do you get immune to it? Living here all the time?"

He thinks for a moment. "Not really. You don't notice it every minute of every day, but there are always these moments—when you're sitting outside after a long day at work, or you're watching your nieces and nephews play at the beach..." he pauses, "when you see a gorgeous woman sitting next to the waterfront..."

I know I'm blushing. And I shouldn't be. I should shut him down with a disapproving glare or something, but oh my. He is hard to resist. Instead I go with a wry smile and one eyebrow lifted.

He chuckles. "Those moments are when you see it like someone new does, and you're reminded all over again that it's one of the most beautiful places on earth, and you're very fortunate to live here."

His gaze is so sultry, and so *genuine*, that I'm desperate to veer away from it. This can't happen, and I can't resist it if I'm trapped in those eyes that are as blue as the ocean he sits next to.

"Where is Christos?" I ask, taking a sip from the soda he brought me.

His eyes lose the softness. "He's waiting for our food." He gestures toward the counter where they ordered. Christos is leaning over it chatting up some girl about our age who's obviously happy to have him flirt with her.

"Does he always do what you tell him?" I ask before I can stop myself.

He twitches a touch, his lips falling into a grim line, stern and unforgiving. This is the other side to the billionaire I think. The part that probably looks exactly like his father. I haven't met the man, but I can imagine that anyone who can manage a multi-billion-dollar company has to be made of steel. Right now, Niko looks made of steel.

"Christos is my deftheri," he says, his voice deep and unforgiving. "It's his job to do what I ask."

"What does that mean? Deftheri?"

His eyes roam out over the ocean next to us and he breathes deeply of the sea air. "It's a counselor, an advisor. Your right-hand man is a term you'd be familiar with. But it's not a job you get paid for, it's a job you're given for life, and it's a great honor in our family."

"He's your consigliere?" I ask, blown away that things like this actually exist—in 2015.

He huffs out a sharp laugh. "You've watched *The Godfather* I guess?"

I nod. "Are you kidding? My dad's a district attorney and my brother is with the FBI. I've watched every organized crime film put out in the last fifty years. And then had to listen to all the things that were unbelievable and wrong with them."

He chuckles. It vibrates through parts of me that it shouldn't and I shift in my seat to tamp down the reaction.

"Wow, so you're from a crime fighting family. That's really interesting. And yes, I guess comparing a deftheri to a consigliere is a good way to get a handle on it. But trust me, it's not related to organized crime. Just an old family tradition."

He pauses as Christos arrives at the table, platters of delicious smelling food in hand. My mouth waters as he sets one in front of me. It has two kabobs of grilled meat on a bed of rice with vegetables, roasted potatoes, and salad. Yum.

"So how long has your brother been with the FBI?" Niko asks as I thank Christos and we all settle in to start eating.

"FBI?" Christos gives me a sharp look.

"Yeah," I smile. Everyone's always so impressed when they hear about Nate. It doesn't bother me at all, I'm really proud of him. "He graduated from Quantico about three years ago. That's the FBI training academy."

I hear Christos mutter something that sounds like, "What are the odds?" but at the same time Niko asks, "Does it scare you? That he might get shot or something?"

I laugh. "No, not at all. He's actually not a field agent. He's an analyst. Sits around at a computer all day tracking hackers and cyber terrorists. It's not too dangerous from what I can tell. The bigger thing for him is that he's responsible for other people's safety. It's hard sometimes. When he has information that he needs to get to a field agent to keep them safe, or he knows something that he can't share with people who could be in danger."

Niko nods around a mouthful of rice pilaf. "That would be rough. Especially if it's people you know—friends from work, that kind of thing."

"The good thing is, other than that though, he loves it."

"And what about your parents?" Niko asks. "Your father's a district attorney?"

"Yes, the Green County District Attorney and my mom's a consultant with the police department."

Christos goes into a coughing fit then, practically spewing fried potatoes all over the table. Niko whacks him on the back, but Christos holds up a hand indicating he's okay, and stands, making his way to the men's room.

After Christos leaves, Niko leans forward and picks up my hand from where it rests on the table. I tense, but don't pull away because I don't want to offend him, and also his skin is warm and it makes my whole arm tingle.

"What do you say we let Christos go on back to work and I'll show you around downtown for a while."

His fingers stroke across my palm and I barely contain the sigh that wants to escape my lips.

I pull my hand away as gently as possible and keep my tone light. "I wouldn't want to hurt his feelings," I say. "He's been talking to me about the big tour since Monday."

A furrow appears between Niko's eyebrows. "Trust me, he won't be offended."

"I don't think it's such a good idea." My heart is pounding, but I don't know whether it's because I'm afraid of him pushing for involvement or because he's so incredibly gorgeous.

"Why not?" He looks at me as though he's trying to solve a puzzle.

"Niko—"

"Do you know that's the first time you've said my name?" he asks. "I like it. Say it again."

I roll my eyes. If only he weren't so damn charming on top of it all.

"Mr. Stephanos—"

"Nooo." He pretends to be wounded in the heart, clutching his chest for all he's worth, head tipped back, eyes screwed shut.

"God, you're impossible." I try to sound stern but don't really pull it off. "Niko then. You know we shouldn't be doing things alone, the two of us, outside the office. If Christos comes with us, that's fine, but otherwise I'll have to decline."

He looks at me like I've grown an extra head. He seems genuinely perplexed. How can he not get this?

"Why?" he asks, face like a little boy's when he's had his favorite toy taken.

"You're my boss," I answer succinctly.

"Ah." He nods. "I see. Let me put your mind at ease then. We don't have the same types of personnel rules here that you're used to in the US. You won't be breaking any laws if you chill with your boss." He leans forward and captures my hand again. "And your boss would very much like to spend some time with you. Preferably alone."

Oh. My. God. Could he get any more inappropriate? Or any hotter? My throat is dry, my armpits are sweating, and I feel like I've run a marathon it's so hard to catch my breath.

I clear my throat. "But that's not true. You do," I say. "It's right in chapter two of your company personnel rules. Page twenty-six in fact."

He starts to chuckle, and before I know it he's outright laughing, his face lighting up, shoulders shaking. I scowl at him, embarrassed, but not sure why. He's the one who doesn't even know his own policies. He should be ashamed. Some CEO he'll be.

Once he gets a grip on himself again he whips off his sunglasses and looks me in the eyes. "Princess. When I had you read those policies it was only to keep you entertained. The fact is, you're probably only the second person to ever read them. That binder has sat there for five years without being touched. My cousin wrote them, and she did it because she was getting an MBA and she needed to do a project for class, so my dad let her write up those policies. They're meaningless."

I stare at him. Uncomprehending. He can't be serious.

"They're not meaningless. They're…" I sputter, searching for the right words. "They're the rules. I mean, rules are the rules. You can't simply decide when you'll follow them and when you won't. If your dad didn't want them followed he wouldn't have had your cousin write them. Or at the very least he wouldn't have gotten them printed up and put into an official manual for employees."

"Look, princess. My dad—" he pauses, seeming to choose his words carefully. "My dad doesn't care what's in that book. He cares about people being happy. As long as everyone's happy he's good with it. And I promise, I'll make sure you stay very happy." He raises an eyebrow at me and even brings out one of the dimples. Fucker.

"No one's going to enforce the so-called rules, therefore they don't matter. I *promise* you, they're meaningless."

My pulse races and I feel a surge of adrenaline that comes not from being turned on, but being angry. Sheer raging pissed. And humiliated. He belittles what I believe in, where I come from. It's part of who I am. My family has devoted their lives to making sure the rules—the laws—are followed. How can he say that's meaningless?

I stand up, leaning over the table as I glare at him. "It must be easy to act like rules are meaningless when you have your daddy's billions behind you," I hiss. "But where I come from we care about things—people, reputations, order, rules. I follow the rules because I can't afford not to. You could never understand that, because you've never been ordinary, but I am. And ordinary people have to do things that billionaires think are *meaningless* every single day."

Then I turn and walk away, vibrating with anger, embarrassment, and the terror that I may have just lost my job.

CHAPTER EIGHT

Niko

ForeignXChange Group

Foster: Word of advice from someone who's been there—don't sleep with your boss. Cheers from Jolly Old England.

The sun is still floating above the horizon when Christos comes out of his room and finds me watching television, shirtless, sprawled across the leather sofa his mother picked out for us when we moved in. I've got a glass of ouzo in my hand and I'm watching the US men's soccer team get their asses handed to them by Argentina.

"No mezedes with that?" Christos asks, eyeing my glass critically.

"Nope," I answer, referring to the fact that I'm not eating the typical olives, seafood and fried appetizers while I drink the ouzo. The shit is powerful and can knock you on your ass when you least expect it. I don't really give a damn right now though. I've been in a stupor for over twenty-four hours. Ever since Tess Richardson said I was spoiled and entitled and didn't understand ordinary people.

"Are you still pouting over that bullshit Tess said to you?" Christos asks as he flops down on the end of the sofa. "She's hot, but she's not worth this. There are plenty of other hot chicks out there. Chicks who won't go all judgmental on you. Who needs that shit anway?"

"You did, apparently, since you were after her too until I told you to back off." I glare at him then turn back to the TV.

He sighs. "Like I said, she's hot. I thought I'd tap that, but I wouldn't have wanted to if I'd known she was such a pain in the ass. Nick," he calls me by the name our soccer teammates in Florida did. "Seriously. Remember who you are, and who she is. That you'd care at all about what she thinks is…well, it's…"

I sit up, tossing back the remainder of the ouzo, then I stand, glowering over him where he lounges on the sofa.

"It's what?" I ask, my voice rough, and my temper rising. "And what the hell do you mean 'who she is and who I am'? Are we too good for college girls now? Or maybe it's American girls? Oh, but wait…did you mean *poor* girls?"

I look down at him, and I see it again, that flash of something foreign, something I never used to notice when he looked at me. I'm not sure what to label it, but it's ugly and dark, and it sets all my nerves on edge.

But as quickly as it appeared, it's gone.

"Bro, I'm sorry," Christos says, standing and tentatively placing a hand on my arm. "I didn't mean to be a dick, I just hate to see you tear yourself up over something a girl you hardly know said in the heat of a moment. All I meant was that she's not from here. She's not one of us, so she doesn't understand who we are—who *you* are. You can't let her lack of understanding get to you. That's why we have the family around us. They understand. They know you. Outsiders will never get it."

This isn't anything new. I've heard variations of this same speech my whole life. Greece is special, Georgios is special, my family is special, and out of my entire family, all the uncles and aunts, cousins, siblings—hell the dogs and cats too—I'm the *most* special. I'm the hope, the future, the darling that everyone attends to. And suddenly, for the first time ever, I'm not sure that what Christos is telling me is right. I'm not sure that I deserve the deference, the preference, all the special treatment. Maybe outsiders don't understand because none of it makes any sense.

I turn away from him now, ready to head to my room for the rest of the night. Everything is jumbled in my head, and the ouzo didn't help matters any.

"Niko." Christos stops me with a hand on my shoulder. "Come out with me tonight. We'll go to the club, have drinks, dance, meet up with some girls. I've heard there's a group of sisters and their friends who are staying at the Anderson villa for the month. I'm sure they'll show up to the club at some point. Fresh tail, a few shots, you'll be good as new." He winks at me. "Say yes."

I think about it for a moment—imagining lying in my bed, pining away over Tess, who I hardly know, and therefore shouldn't really care about this much. My chest hurts, and all I want is the oblivion that more ouzo will bring. Too much alcohol and pounding bass might drown out the voices in my head—Tess's voice in my head—nothing else has during the last twenty-four hours.

"Fine," I say. "But call my dad's house and get a car sent up. I'm drinking until I pass out."

Christos grins. "That's my boy," he jokes, slapping me on the back. I don't return the smile.

"I'll be ready at nine," I tell him. Then I head to the kitchen for the ouzo and a clean glass. Let the road to oblivion begin.

**

When we stumble into the club it's nearly ten, and I'm feeling lighter than air, like I might float away. It's the ouzo. It's a different drunk than other hard alcohols or beer give me. I don't always like it, but tonight it's exactly what the doctor ordered.

"Which waitress do you want?" Christos asks. He's been exceptionally attentive tonight, making sure the car was stocked with ouzo and ice, telling the driver to take us around the island for thirty minutes while we drank more and he called some of the girls we know who are always up to party. I didn't have the heart to tell him I'm drinking tonight not scoring. I can't imagine screwing one of the usual party girls right now. My head's too mixed up.

"I don't give a shit," I mumble at him as I stagger toward the staircase to the VIP area. I'm not surprised to see that Christos has appropriated the entire area. Only our closest friends and cousins are sitting up there. I take my usual place at the table with the best view of the floor. In mere seconds one of the waitresses is there, fawning over me. I switch from ouzo to scotch and ignore her otherwise.

Christos brings over a couple of girls along with our cousins Marco and Dmitri. They're a few years older than us and work in the operations division—meaning they deal with the actual ships and equipment we need to run the company. Big shit. Maintenance, acquisitions. I'm scheduled to take over that division as COO next year sometime when my great uncle retires.

My three cousins and the two chicks they're with try to jostle me out of my ill temper for a while, but when I don't respond, they leave me alone, continuing some dumbass drinking game Christos has devised that insures the girls will have to take turns removing bits of clothing. I can't see it lasting long as neither of them was wearing much to begin with.

I let the scotch slide down my throat, burning its way into my consciousness along with the words that Tess spoke to me. I know it shouldn't matter—*she* shouldn't matter—but somehow she does. That she thinks so little of me—a girl I immediately admired so much—is painful. And I can't help but wonder how much of what she said is true. And if it is, how much should I care?

The dancers on the floor below me bump and grind to the techno music, bodies winding together like some sort of animal with hundreds of legs and heads. It's nearly impossible to make out an individual person in the chaos, but my eyes are drawn to a figure in white, her undulating form like a vision in a fantasy. She's pressed against a guy dressed all in black, so her fair hair and white dress stand out, and even from this distance I can see that she's not completely steady on her feet. I think the guy might be holding her up as much as dancing with her.

I continue to watch them, fascinated by the way her golden hair shimmies with her body, and how her legs look in the sky high platform heels, when the music breaks before the drop, and she tosses her head back for a split second, her hair falling away from her face at the same time. It's Tess. Fucking Tess. The Tess who handed me my ass yesterday. The Tess who has haunted my every waking moment since.

I'm on my feet before I even realize it. Moving away from the table toward the staircase to the dance floor.

"What's going on, Niko?" Christos calls from behind me. I wave my arm over my head to let him know it's all good, and keep moving.

When I reach the floor, my drunk mind is momentarily confused by the chaos of the pounding bass and gyrating bodies, but somewhere in the back of my head I must have a Tess compass, because it only takes me a few seconds to orient myself and remember which part of the room I saw her in.

As usual, the crowds part to let me through, and when they don't a quick tap on someone's shoulder does the trick. Before I know it I'm standing next to the guy who's dancing with her, and I lean down and say in his ear, "I want to cut in."

He looks up at me, confusion clouding his face. He's not anyone I know, probably a tourist or summer resident. Tess hasn't noticed that I'm here, and his hands are still on her hips as she moves to the music. I glance down at them wrapped around her tiny frame and have the urge to peel his fingers back as far as they'll go—then a touch farther—one at a time until he's no longer touching her, and as a bonus, is screaming in pain.

"Uh, you her boyfriend or something, man?" he asks.

"Yeah. I am," I say. Whatever will get him away from her the fastest.

He looks me up and down once, obviously calculating that I'm the bigger guy, then steps away, giving me a little salute before he moves on to another girl dancing with her friends a few feet away. I slide into his spot, right as Tess turns to see where the hands that were all over her a moment ago have gone.

I can tell that she's been drinking, her lids are heavy and her cheeks are flushed. She jerks in surprise when she sees me, but I put my hands on her waist and pull her gently back into me, lowering my head to her shoulder where I say, "Don't think, just dance with me for a minute." My voice is rough, and I feel her shiver when I hold her. I can't help but notice that her hair smells like cinnamon, and it's silky on my cheek as I start to sway with her.

I move my hands around to her front, placing them flat against her abs. She's so tiny that my thumbs reach to the bottom of her breasts and I can't stop myself from moving them along the plump curve that rests there. She sighs and arches back against me, forcing her delectable ass into my groin, which hardens immediately.

As the bass continues to thump and the lights flash blue and red, blinking off and on, strobing one minute and sweeping the room in the next, I hold Tess flush against me and we move together like two pieces of a puzzle. I bend my knees and grind against her ass, not caring in the slightest if she feels that I'm as hard as a chunk of concrete. I bury my nose in her hair and breathe deep, whispering my lips up the side of her silky neck.

After a few minutes I'm so hot I'm afraid I might blow my load right on the dance floor. I'm drunk, and angry, and more turned on than I've ever been in my life, and it's all because of this woman. She's making me crazy and if I don't have her soon I might explode.

I lean down again and say, "Come with me," as I grab her wrist and pull her along behind me, moving off the dance floor and into a back hallway of the club, where the offices and storage rooms are.

She follows, without resisting, but I can feel her stumble a couple of times, and it reminds me that she's obviously been drinking. It probably doesn't take much at her size.

I stop, putting her back to the wall and facing her while I keep ahold of both her hands

"Hi," she says, her cheeks pink and smooth.

"Hi," I whisper, leaning my forehead against hers while I try to catch my breath. I'm not sure what I'm doing here, but she makes me feel better, and I've felt really crappy since yesterday, so I'm going with it.

After a moment I raise my head, looking her in the eyes. "Who are you here with?"

"My roommate and her boyfriend," she answers, not returning my gaze.

"Tess," I say, putting a fingertip under her chin so she's forced to look at me. "I'm sorry I made you angry yesterday."

She nods. "I'm sorry I was so hard on you." She pauses, then continues, "But you need to understand that I have a lot riding on my internship. I can't afford to stay here if I don't have it, and if I can't stay here it sets me back a whole semester in school. That's another semester of student loans, another semester of not earning an income, not to mention I would have missed out on the opportunity to live here and get the professional experience at Stephanos."

I'm still lightheaded, and now my dick aches to boot, but I watch the earnestness in her eyes, and something inside of me hurts in a way I've never hurt before. I smooth back a lock of her hair that's fallen over her forehead.

"I want you to do your internship, Tess. I can tell already that you're smart and good at what you do. Everyone's told me you're a great addition to the department. Can't you trust me to keep something between us separate from the job?"

"Trust you?" Her voice is sharp, but her expression is pleading. "I don't even *know* you," she says, "and what I've heard isn't too promising."

That snaps me to attention.

"What exactly have you heard?"

"I'm not going to name names, but your reputation at the office isn't spotless."

Juliet. I sigh. I probably deserve this. I shouldn't have threatened her job. I had no intention of firing her anyway, I was trying to get her to back off, and it seemed like the most expedient way to do it. Dumbass move.

I lean into Tess, rubbing my cheek along hers, and I feel her sink into me. She wants this too, if I can only get her to admit it.

"I've made some mistakes, but I learn from them. I absolutely can keep work and personal separate, and that's a promise I've never made to anyone before, because I didn't realize it might be necessary. Now I know it is. Come on, you want to get to know me. You do. And I want to get to know you. In every way possible," I murmur. "Outside the office. Let's see what happens."

She gives me a little shove and I back off an inch or two so I can see her face. Her lips tremble. "Please," she whispers. "I can't. Please don't make me."

Everything inside of me goes stone cold. My heart stops, my limbs freeze, my mind is numb. I step back, shaking my head slowly to try and clear it. *Make* her? Fuck. Is that what she feels like? Like I'm forcing myself on her? My stomach lurches and I stumble, putting a hand out to the wall behind me in order to steady myself.

I look at her, shaking my head again. "You can't think...I would never..." My voice is weak and my chest burns, because while I may be an asshole, and I'm not above trying to entice a woman to sleep with me, I would never, ever force myself on one. A guy tried to rape one of my sisters once, and I'll never forget what she was like for months afterwards. The way my parents looked as they dealt with the police and lawyers. No, I like my partners just that—partners. Willing, enthusiastic, and active.

I look back at Tess, and I think she's as horrified by the whole concept as I am. Her hands are over her mouth like she's trying to capture something that's fighting to get out. Something even more vile than what's floating in front of us—in between us.

"I'm sorry," she finally blurts out before she turns and runs down the hall back to the dance floor.

I lean against the wall, my head thrown back and my legs weak. I'm motionless for long minutes, as I contemplate what she's said, what she's opened my eyes to. I'm rich—filthy rich—and even though I'm used to that and don't think much of it, the odds of Tess having ever known or worked for a billionaire are slim to absofuckinglutely no way. I'm her boss yeah, but more importantly, my father owns the company. She's in a foreign country, no family, hardly any friends. She doesn't speak the language, she doesn't understand the culture, and if what she said is true, she needs the money my family provides her to live here for the next year.

It all becomes glaringly clear, like a flashlight has shined on a whole corner of the room I didn't even realize existed. What the fuck was I thinking? Of course she can't get involved with me. Of course she feels pressured, of course I'm a selfish asshole for hitting on her. I press back against the wall and swear.

I'm an idiot of the highest order, and I've scared the crap out of a smart, beautiful, ambitious young woman who is relying on my family to protect her and keep her safe while she's here in Georgios. Even after my father warned me, I've kept pursuing her. He'd be really pissed if he knew, and I should be ashamed of myself.

I push off the wall. She was right, I am selfish. I don't know the first thing about what normal people deal with, and it's embarrassing. I should. I should understand how my employees live and how they view me. The fact that I don't tells me I'm nowhere near ready to run this company.

An idea begins to form in my mind. I need a crash course on normal, lessons on what life is like for average working people—the people who work for me. I need to be tutored in how the real world works, and I'm hoping that I haven't offended Tess so badly that she won't be willing to help me. As much as I want Tess Richardson, I *need* her more. I need her to teach me how to be a better man. I need her to be my friend.

CHAPTER NINE

ForeignXChange Group

Tess: Hey, Foster. What's your favorite part of England? I love fish and chips. I know they're not good for me, but sometimes I think the extra weight and clogged arteries would totally be worth it if I could have a non-stop buffet of fish and chips.

As I lie in bed after getting home from the nightclub, I think back to the way Niko's lips felt as they coasted along my cheek and neck. The way his hands felt as they stroked the underside of my breasts. The way his voice sounded, all coffee grounds rough when he spoke in my ear—hot breath, hotter words. I wiggle in my bed, an ache blooming between my thighs. Cass and

Anton dropped me off before they went home to his place, so I'm alone, and I'm hurting—emotionally, mentally, physically.

Saying no to Niko might be the hardest thing I've ever had to do. I want him something crazy. But I'm a smart girl, and my head always rules my heart, or in this case, my hormones. It was rough though. That's why I was nearly begging him to stop tempting me. I knew if he pressed one more minute I'd give in and then what a mess I would have made of my life.

I'm not poor, I know this. In the grand scheme of things I'm very fortunate. I have a loving family who have reliable jobs, we have good healthcare and a nice house. Nothing fancy, but all of it comfortable and safe. Things like private college and study abroad however, are not in my parents' budget. I've had to borrow and work and save for what I've done in college, and getting out in four years is part of the plan, so that I don't go any further into debt than I have to.

I know Niko can't understand that. I know I was hard on him yesterday, but he needs to accept that he is a risk I can't take, no matter how many times he promises it won't impact my job. Yesterday he was so mired in getting his way he couldn't seem to absorb it. Tonight he was different. I'm not sure if it was all the alcohol I'd had—and I'm guessing by the foggy look in his eyes he was far from sober too—but he was a kinder, gentler Niko. Also a sexier one. The way he seemed to breathe me in, it was like I had some special quality that he needed. Like I was a form of sustenance to him.

I thrash on my bed again, the alcohol is wearing off and I'm frustrated and sad. It took every bit of willpower I could dig up to turn him away. I close my eyes and feel him. Niko Stephanos might be the sexiest man I've ever seen, and I told him no. Maybe I've lost my mind. Maybe I'm going to spend an entire year in Greece sexually frustrated, beating myself up about missed opportunities.

"Aaargh!" I yell into the dark of my room before I flop over on my stomach. I slip my hand into my panties and press on my damp, hot clit. I should have taken that discussion about vibrators I had with Cass more seriously. It's going to be a very long year.

**

Monday morning is my first day of classes. From now on I'll be at classes in the mornings and working at Stephanos in the afternoons. It's a relief to go to class. School is what I know best, and the American University here is small, easy to navigate, but interesting, with students from all over the world. Classes are taught in English, and by lunchtime I've made friends with a pair of girls from Germany, Cristal and Una. They're both tall and blonde, and I feel like a twelve year old next to their Amazonian bodies, but they're funny, and they've invited me to go on a boat trip with a bunch of other students this weekend. In the meantime, we all go to lunch at the student union building.

"Do you think they'd let us have some more of this fig stuff?" Una asks, scarfing down a mouthful of fruit salad.

"Here." I slide my plate over to her. "Not a fan of figs—unless they're wrapped in bacon."

"Yum, thank you," she mumbles between bites.

"I wish you didn't have to go to work right after lunch," Cristal pouts. "Una and I are going downtown to shop, and then we're spending a couple of hours at the beach with these guys we met at a bar last night. There's four of them, so it's not like you'd be a fifth wheel or anything."

"Show her the picture," Una instructs, and Cristal takes out her phone, clicking to a photo that she holds up. It's of her and Una with four very cute men, everyone smiling and holding up their Greek and German beers.

"This is last night at the bar," Cristal says.

"They look like fun guys, but I can't miss work."

Una shrugs, but Cristal looks sad. "You have so many classes and so many hours at your internship when are you ever going to be able to enjoy being abroad?" she asks.

I flinch. She's not the first one to say it to me. Cass has also wondered why I'm so overscheduled for a study abroad program. What none of them understand is that it's to keep from having to pay tuition another semester. I'm trying my hardest to finish in four years, and also get real job experience so that I'm spared the fate of most recent college grads—working at Starbucks.

"I've got a plan," I say. "And in order to achieve it I can't afford to go without taking a full load of classes and getting the work experience."

Una shakes her head. "Someone really needed to explain the idea of study abroad to you. It's not about having plans, or meeting goals or getting experience inside a stale old office. You're supposed to be soaking up the local culture, learning the language, enjoying your youth."

Cristal laughs, "Leave her be. She'll do all of it in her own time, and her own way." I'm grateful for her taking the pressure off of me, but I can't help but wonder if Una's right. Am I letting an opportunity pass me by because I'm working so hard to be proactive, to plan for my future? Maybe sometimes you can be so focused on the future you don't notice your present?

**

I'm standing in front of the Stephanos offices and I'm so nervous I've broken out in a sweat. I have no idea what Niko thought of me running off at the club this weekend. Following so closely on the heels of our disagreement Friday at lunch, I'm expecting that he's not too pleased. But at least if he tries to fire me now I don't have to have the additional humiliation of having slept with him. I don't need that on my conscience, or in the company's personnel records.

The front door to the building opens and Santo, the security guard who mans the lobby, pokes his head out. His accent is heavy, but like all the Stephanos employees he speaks enough English to do basic business.

"Miss," he says, smiling. "You ready to come in?"

I start walking the last few steps toward the door. "Yes, Santo, I'm sorry, I was distracted." I give him what I hope is a normal smile to counteract my crazy—standing in front of the building staring at it for five minutes.

"It's good," he answers as he holds the door open for me to walk through. "Mr. Niko asks you to go to his office first thing."

My heart double pumps in my chest. "Um, okay. Did he say why?" I ask, swallowing my fear.

"No. Only to have you go to him right away. I've been watching for you."

I nod. "Great. Thank you, Santo."

He gives me a little tip of his hat and I make my way through the lobby, cold dread lodging itself in my gut like a chunk of ice.

When I get to the finance offices Juliet gives me the once over then announces with a look of pity, "Mr. Stephanos needs to see you immediately."

I grit my teeth and try to sound polite. "Yes, Santo told me. Thank you."

She rolls her eyes and I move on by, dropping my purse in my desk drawer before I go to Niko's office and knock.

"Come in," his deep voice calls out. I stifle a shiver that's a strange mixture of fear and excitement before I turn the knob and walk through.

He's sitting at his desk with the view of the water behind him. His ebony hair is a touch too long, curling up on the edges, and he's wearing a blue dress shirt today, sleeves rolled up as usual. Its cut narrow, showcasing his broad shoulders and muscled torso. When his head lifts and I meet his blue eyes, sparkling in all of that Mediterranean gold skin, he nearly takes my breath away. Niko Stephanos is who the term "Greek god" was coined for.

His lips slide into a soft smile when he sees me. "You're here," he says as if he wasn't sure I would be.

"Yes, I should be here by one most days. My classes are all in the mornings."

He walks out from behind his desk, smiling warmly, but not coming too close. "Please, come have a seat." He walks to the sitting area in his office and gestures to the sofa. I comply, sitting on the edge and folding my hands on my knees primly. He's acting very strange, so I prepare to get fired, my head is buzzing and I'm fighting to stay professional, but I really want to cry.

He clears his throat, looking down for a minute before he pins me with those baby blues and my damn traitorous heart flutters in spite of how uncomfortable I am.

"I owe you an apology," he says before pausing and running a hand through his hair. "I thought about what you said to me the other night, and I realized that you're absolutely right. I've been unfair to you, I haven't treated you the way I should treat my staff, and I'm truly sorry for that."

I stare at him, not sure what to say now. I'm still back at being fired, my mind hasn't caught up yet.

As if sensing I'm unable to speak, he continues. "I have spent most of my life in a very protected and narrow world. There are a lot of traditions in my family, certain ways things are done, certain things that are expected of the oldest son. What it all boils down to is that I've been given everything I wanted, and surrounded by people who live in the same world I do."

I nod my head, to encourage him to continue. I'm breathless from the honesty he's giving me, the view into his private self that I haven't done a damn thing to deserve.

"When I realized the position I'd put you in this last week—" he stops, a blush rising to his perfectly stubbled cheeks, "—I was ashamed of myself. You were right, I don't know what the people around me are thinking, or what their lives are like. I've been coddled and sheltered for far too long."

Guilt cascades through me. I got pissed, gave the guy a hard time, and sent him into an existential crisis. "I never meant to judge you," I say.

"But you were right," he interrupts. "Everything you said was right, and even though my family spoils me, my father would never condone me harassing an employee. In fact, I have to be truthful and admit he's asked me *not* to date them. One of the things we pride ourselves on in this company is taking care of our own. A good percentage of the employees are family, and the rest we treat that way. You're a good employee, Tess. I'd like a second chance to be the kind of boss you deserve."

He finishes by flashing that smile at me, the one that makes me doubt turning him down, though I know I didn't have a choice.

"Thank you," I tell him, not admitting that a part of me will miss Niko the cad.

"I'm wondering if you might be willing to do a special project with me?" he asks.

I raise an eyebrow.

"It's personal, but not the way you're thinking." He takes a deep breath and I realize that he's nervous about this. Who'd have thought the hot billionaire could be nervous about anything? "I want to be better—more in sync with the rest of the world. I need to understand the way normal people live. It'll make me a better boss, and

I have a feeling a better person too." He gives me an adorable little shrug and smile and I groan to myself. Shit. Who is this all-new sweeter Niko? He melts my heart as much as alpha billionaire Niko melts my panties.

"I think that's great," I tell him, trying to sound encouraging since I'm not yet sure why he's telling me all of this.

"And," he pauses, his jaw flexing for a moment, "I want you to help me."

What? He has to be joking. I find myself looking around the room as if there might be someone else there he could be talking to. "Um…"

He chuckles. "You're real, Tess. You have a real life. Real friends. You're not related to me, you're not Greek, you're not impressed by all my crap. You weren't afraid to give it to me straight, and I'm grateful for that. You're the perfect person to help me get a much-needed dose of reality. I'm hoping we can be friends and you'll show me the ropes."

"You're serious?" I ask.

He nods, hopeful smile in place. God, he's so beautiful. It should be against the law for a man to look like him.

I give myself a mental shake. He's asking for my help. He's asking me to be his friend. I need to get the hell over my superficial appreciation of his looks and help him.

"So, the poor little rich boy needs a buddy, huh?" I temper the harsh words with a soft tone and a genuine smile.

He laughs softly. "Something like that." He looks at me, intensity in his eyes. "Will you do it?"

Can I do this? Can I be nothing more than friends with my boss, a super hot Greek billionaire who sends my girl parts into a frenzy every time he looks at me? For whatever reason, I want to. I want to help him, I want to know him better. So I tamp down the misgivings about my ability to ignore my attraction and grin. "Yes. It would be my pleasure to be your real friend. I would love to show you what we regular people do with our lives." I think for a moment. "But didn't you go to college in Miami? I would have thought you'd have gotten a taste of the real world then?"

He huffs out a breath and grimaces. "You would think. However, my father has a house in Miami Beach. Christos and I lived there. We also had a ship docked at the private marina, and a jet on call twenty-four seven at the airport." He shakes his head. "I used to fly the soccer team to away games in it, so we wouldn't have to ride buses."

I stare at him. "You're kidding."

He stares back. "No."

I can't help but smile at the ridiculousness of it all. "God, you really do need me," I finally say.

He breathes deeply as if relief has enabled his lungs to work again. "Thank you," he says. "Thank you for forgiving me and for agreeing to help me."

"You're welcome."

"So what should my first assignment be?" he asks, excitement weaving its way through his deep voice giving me a glimpse at Niko as a boy. Darling.

"Um, I'm not sure. You want to do my laundry tonight?"

He laughs. Guess he's not ready to get that real.

I think for a moment—something real, safe, fun. Then I have it. "I was invited to a boat party with some other kids from school this weekend."

He raises an eyebrow at me. "I've been to a few boat parties in my lifetime," he says, sarcastically.

"On anything smaller than that yacht in Miami?" I ask.

He clears his throat. "Well…"

"Ha! As I thought. This is a rental because we're all from somewhere else, and it's tiny because we don't have enough money to get the bigger one. If you come you have to chip in ten Euros for the rental and bring your own beer."

He looks at me like he's trying to keep from laughing.

"I'm serious rich boy. No champagne, no having your staff pack caviar for your lunch. In fact, I'll handle lunch if you buy the beer. And it needs to be beer that a regular person can afford. Whatever the Greek equivalent of Bud Light is."

"Good God," he sighs dramatically. "You're going to kill me before we even get started."

I stand and point a finger at him. "I'm a tough teacher, so if you want to do this you're going to have to suck it up, buttercup. I mean it. A six-pack of cheap beer, a towel, your swimsuit. That's all. I'll bring your lunch and meet you at the marina at ten on Saturday morning."

He stands and salutes me. "Yes, ma'am, you're the boss."

I cock my head and inspect him for a moment. "I'm proud of you," I say. "You're going to make a great regular guy."

The look he gives me is almost tender, and I blink a couple of times before I mumble some goodbyes and hustle out of his office.

When I get back to my desk and sit down for the first time in hours, I slump back in my chair and try to do nothing but breathe for a few minutes. Friends. Niko Stephanos and me. What have I done?

CHAPTER TEN

Niko

ForeignXChange Group

Paisley: Waves from Russia. Hi everyone! It's super cold here, and I haven't gone to any parties or met any boys, but Russia is beautiful and I'm working at the Hermitage with some of the most famous art historians in the world. I feel like I'm learning about a whole new world. It's amazing.

I feel lighter. Lighter than I've felt in months, and all because Tess Richardson has agreed to be my friend. Or mentor. Something like that. I'm enthralled with the idea of being a normal guy. The kind of guy who gets to spend time with girls like Tess.

And I want to be the best student she's ever had—maybe I'm the only student she's ever had, but why not set the bar high? I want to show her that I'm taking this seriously and to do that I need a plan.

I start in the place where I spend the most time—Stephanos Shipping. In order to understand my average employees better I need to actually see some of them. Up until now, I've spent all my time with the heads of the various departments in the financial section. I know them. I know their assistants, I know a handful of other senior level staff. That means there are dozens of workers who are under my supervision that I've rarely met, and almost never talked to.

That changes now.

I begin by asking Annais to get me the schedules for all of the staff meetings my department heads hold with their own staff. The list is daunting, but I decide to do one a week come rain or shine, and that insures I'll be done at the end of the calendar year.

I also decide to take any opportunity I can find to visit other parts of the company, and meet regular staff members. So when I find the scrap of paper with the number of the tanker ship I saw being mysteriously loaded, I decide that instead of having Annais call down to ask about it, I'll walk to the shipping dock myself.

I walk into the shipping office that sits next to the docks, and no one is at the front desk. This is the nuts and bolts part of our operation, although the office here in Georgios is much smaller than most due to our limited traffic in and out of port.

I can hear noise from the back of the building, so I swing around behind the counter and make my way past the bare bones cubicles set up for the agents to log shipments into our databases. Then I walk through a set of double swinging doors to the back warehouse where smaller items that are shipped can be stored. The big shipping containers and tanks are kept in the yard outside.

When I walk in everyone is bustling around, moving crates identical to those I saw being loaded onto the tanker. No one notices me for a moment, and I absentmindedly brush off the dust on a crate next to me.

"Mr. Stephanos!" the head shipping clerk cries out as she sees me standing there.

"Magda." I smile as I stride toward her and put out my hand. Her eyes dart around nervously for a moment, and I wonder why a woman who's known me since I was old enough to toddle would be anxious to see me. I take her hand in both of mine and lean forward to kiss her on each cheek. "You're looking as beautiful as ever," I say.

She blushes and rolls her eyes. "You need to stop teasing old ladies, Mr. Niko," she tells me. Then she pats my cheek. "But look at that beautiful face." She keeps ahold of my hand and begins to walk us up to the front counter, chattering the whole time. The other workers keep their heads down, moving the crates from the warehouse to a trolley outside that will take them to the ship. As we leave the warehouse I look down at the crate next to me and notice Syria as a destination on the manifest.

"Now," Magda says to me as we reach the front office and she sits on her stool behind the counter. "Tell me what brings you down here. You could have called you know."

I give her my most innocent smile and shrug. "I need to get out of the office more, Magda. And I missed you. We haven't had a company dinner in so long how else will I get to see you if I don't come down here?"

"Oh, Mr. Niko. Next time you call and I will come up to see you. I'll bring you some spanakopita that I make with my special recipe, yes?"

"That would be great," I say, thinking that if there's food as a payoff I should have been visiting the regular staff a lot more often.

"Now. What did you need?" she asks.

I snap back to the task at hand. "I have a question— about a shipment I saw being loaded."

She nods and taps at the keyboard for her computer.

I pull out the note I wrote with the ship's number and the date. "It was a tanker, 430072, on the eighteenth. The guys were loading crates that looked a lot like the ones you have in back now. I couldn't understand why they'd be putting crates on a tanker. Do we normally transport things other than liquids on those ships?"

She clicks away on the computer and then says, "Ah, yes. Here it is." She turns the monitor toward me so I can see the screen. "On the eighteenth that ship was loaded with medical supplies."

I squint at the information. A huge tanker, capable of carrying half a million barrels of oil was used to transport twenty crates, each less than eight feet square? Crates with what? Bandages and aspirin?

"What types of medical supplies?" I ask.

"It doesn't say here. They're usually medicines—" She seems to search for a word or idea. "Some kind of medicines I think."

I nod, still wholly unconvinced. "Where did it come from and where was it going?"

She points to the screen again. "Los Angeles to Syria."

Okay, medical supplies to a war-torn country. Nothing odd about that. They didn't come from here though. We have medical supplies shipped into Georgios, not out. We certainly shouldn't be taking the extra time and manpower to unload those crates from one ship here and load them onto another only to send them one to Syria. It's a short trip, they should have kept right on going and delivered before turning around and docking here.

But, shipping routes aren't Magda's purview, only shipping records, so I give her my most benevolent smile and make a mental note to investigate this further. This looks like someone is trying to pad the shipping costs, and if that padding weren't on the records, they could be pocketing the extra fee. That could add up really fast. Meaning someone or several someones could be getting wealthy off of my company. I grit my teeth. That can't continue.

"Thank you for the information, Magda," I say, squeezing her hand in mine. I haven't gotten a chance to chat with the workers in the warehouse, but I can tell that Magda will think it's odd if I try. Time to go. My visit's left me with more questions than it's answered I'm afraid.

"Next time you call and I'll bring you the spanakopita!" Magda calls out as I leave the office. If only spanakopita could help me become who Tess wants me to be.

**

"What's on the agenda this weekend?" Christos asks me as we play Xbox in our living room after work.

"I've got plans on Saturday and then Sunday I really ought to go to church. My mom is going to start sending my sisters over here to embarrass me into it soon."

His eyes dart between me and the game. "What plans do you have on Saturday? Did you hook up with someone I don't know about?"

I shrug and blast my way through a wall on screen. "No. I'm actually going out on the water with Tess and some of her friends from school."

He sits up straighter, hitting pause on the game console. "No shit? So you are going to hit that after all?"

I restart the game and roll my eyes. "No, asshole, I'm not going to 'hit that'. We're friends and she invited me to go along as a gesture—of *friendship*."

Christos snorts. "Why the hell would you want to be *friends* with her? I mean, she's hot to look at, but she's wound pretty tight."

God. When did my cousin get to be such a jerk? I swallow, trying to absorb and diffuse some of the anger that rolls over me.

"And so, what? If she's not going to fuck me then why would I bother with her?" I grit out, holding the trigger as I mow down half a village with machine gun fire.

He sighs, the impatience in his demeanor obvious from three feet away.

"I get that you like her or whatever, but really, if you're not going to sleep with her why would you want to hang out? I mean, she's the daughter of middle-class cops in Illinois for fuck's sake, she can't be that interesting."

I'll admit it, I've never had a friend who's a girl. I've hooked up, dated here and there, and mostly partied, nothing too serious ever crossing my radar, and I've never met a girl who interested me much beyond sex. But I'd like to think that I wouldn't choose any friend, girl or otherwise, based on what their family does for a living. The idea that Christos thinks I would or should is insulting.

"First of all, like I said, we're *friends*, there's no reason why where she comes from should matter." My voice is louder than it should be and I've got one of my fists clenched around the gaming controller so tightly it aches. "Secondly, she's smart and she's got more integrity in her little finger than half the people I know. Since when did having a profession where you help people and uphold the law become something to be ashamed of? She's proud of her family and I think she has every right to be."

"Oh, please," he scoffs. "Cops are fine, but they don't matter to people like us. They're there to serve the masses. In our world law enforcement's a nuisance but that's about all."

As the words tumble out of Christos's mouth, something inside of me spikes, something sharp and quick and sickening. I'm not angry anymore, I'm beyond that—I'm confused, and disgusted, and even sad. Sad that after twenty-four years side by side, I suddenly feel like I don't know Christos at all.

I stare at him, trying to figure out where this man came from, and where the one I grew up with has gone.

"So you're saying we're above the law? That being wealthy makes us so special that we shouldn't have to live by the same laws as everyone else?"

He pins me with a laser glare for a brief moment. "Yeah, that's exactly what I'm saying."

"What the hell is the matter with you?"

He starts to laugh like he's going to blow me off. I grab the front of his shirt and yank him once before letting go with a shove.

"No, really, Christos. Who the fuck are you right now? We have money, and yeah that makes us different than the majority of people, but it doesn't mean we've got a free ticket to live however we want." I stand and pace a couple of times in front of him, clawing a hand through my hair. "That isn't how we were raised. My dad would kick your ass if he heard you talk like that. It goes against everything Stephanos Shipping stands for. Breaking a few rules is one thing, but we don't break the *law*, not in my company."

His expression is hard as he turns to me, nose to nose. I've never seen his eyes so cold, his lips press together in one thin line. He answers me in a low gravelly voice, and if I didn't know better, I'd think that I see loathing in his eyes when he speaks to me.

"*Your* company. That's right, I almost forgot, what with all the things I do for *your* company that you haven't got a clue about. But see, that's my job. I'm the guy that does what has to be done so the prince doesn't get his pretty hands dirty. I take it all on, I do every bit of it, for *you*. And you have no idea *how* it gets done, or *that* it gets done, or by *whom*."

He steps around me, shaking his head. "That's okay, man. You go on your little trip with the cop's daughter, and cling to your illusions of how much like everyone else we are. When she's done with you, I'll still be here—your deftheri—because that's for life."

He swings on his heel and stalks out of the room, leaving me alone, confused, and worried that somehow my life isn't what it looks like.

CHAPTER ELEVEN

Tess

ForeignXChange Group

Tess: How much money do you guys spend each week on food and incidentals? I swear Greece is the most expensive place I've ever seen. I can't figure out where all my money goes.

The days fly by with the combination of school and work. I'm running from first thing in the morning until late at night, and I only see Niko in passing, but I assure him that I'm expecting him to be at the boat party, and he seems to be excited about it.

By Thursday afternoon I'm beginning to wilt, the nonstop pace wearing me down along with the stress of dealing with a different country, culture and language.

While in most of the places I spend time my lack of Greek isn't a big problem, there are still plenty of situations each day where I'm stymied, unable to do some of the most basic things, such as shop for groceries or find the right bus route.

I've been in the midst of one of those situations for the last twenty minutes as I attempt to communicate via phone with another Stephanos employee who works out of the Athens office. While she speaks English, it's kitchen English—where's the bathroom, how much does this cost, the dress is blue—and her heavy accent makes it more difficult to understand her.

I've called her in the first place because there are discrepancies in the account I'm working on. The records show one column for what the company shipped, one column for what that shipment cost, and then another column for what the company has paid to Stephanos. There is a code that goes with the shipments and is attached to the payments as well. From what I can tell, the company whose account I'm working on has been paying nothing for their shipments. But there's a special code for all of their business, and I'm sure that will explain it, if I can just get someone to tell me what the code stands for.

"I understand that there's a set of letters and numbers for every type of shipment," I say loudly and slowly as if I'm talking to a very elderly person. "I need to know what this set is for. What type of shipment uses this set of letters and numbers? Can you help me with that?"

The woman in Athens responds with a tone of exasperation. "I tell you miss, no code. No shipment. I'm sorry. It does not exist here."

I finally give up and end the call. "Argh!" I groan in frustration as I throw my head back in my desk chair and screw my eyes shut.

"Problems?"

I open my eyes to find Christos laughing at me.

I smile. He's a charming guy, good looking, and carefree. And best of all, we aren't attracted to each other in the slightest, so it's easy to be around him, unlike his magnetic cousin.

"I'm experiencing a bit of a language barrier with the Athens office, and I can't figure something out on the account I'm assigned to."

"Ah. The Athens office. Let me guess, Laurinda? In receiving?"

"Oh my gosh, yes! How did you know?"

He chuckles before sitting at the small armchair facing my desk. "She's famous for her English skills that disappear every time any employee who hasn't been with the company for at least twenty-five years calls. She was hired by my Uncle Ari in the dark ages when there were three people in the Athens office, and they all spoke Greek. Once the company grew to such gargantuan international proportions and everyone started speaking English to conduct business, she suddenly became monolingual."

"Well, she's a cranky old woman in any language."

Christos laughs again. "But maybe I can help you with whatever you're trying to figure out. I don't know everything, but I've been around the division for a couple of years now, so I've picked up a few things."

"Would you?" I ask, feeling the first bit of hope I've had all afternoon. "It's this first account on the list. I'm supposed to be doing the quarterly report on it.

Everything seems to make sense until I get to the actual money received. There is none, and there's this weird code in the last column that I can't find anywhere in the code book."

I turn the printout of the spreadsheet toward Christos so he can look at it, but he never even glances down, just pulls it from my hand, his mouth set in a grim line that's so unlike him.

"Oh, yeah," he says, folding the paper in half quickly. "This is one of our special accounts. You should have never been given this one, that was our mistake."

"Oh." I'm suddenly confused. I've been working on this account for two weeks, and neither Niko nor Annais said anything.

"No worries," Christos says, "just send me whatever work you've done on it and I'll have one of our senior accountants finish up the report. Let me tell Annais to get you a different account. Are you working on any others?" he asks, standing and tapping the folded paper against his leg. He's trying to seem casual, but I can tell he's agitated.

"This is the one I started on, but I have three others on my list."

"Great." He gives me a tight smile. "Send me those as well and I'll make sure they're not any of our special accounts too. If they're good to go I'll send them back to you. If not, I'll have Annais replace them."

"Oh, okay. Thank you, Christos. If you hadn't stopped by I might have been struggling with this for days. It seemed like no one knew what the heck those codes were." I smile at him and he nods his head.

"Happy to help," he answers. "And if you ever find anything like that again, come to me right away. There are all kinds of special circumstances that Annais won't know about that I do. And Niko's too busy to be bothered with those things, so I'm your go-to guy, yeah?"

"Definitely. Thanks again."

After Christos leaves, I open my email and forward the list of the other accounts to him along with the file from the account I've been working on, then I go to the copy room and assemble some reports that Annais said we'll need for our weekly staff meeting.

When I get back to my desk I realize that I've given Christos all of my work. I'm sitting at the office without any projects and Annais is gone all afternoon. I decide to check out the other accounts I was assigned but hadn't started on yet. I know what those special codes look like now, so I should be able to tell if they're the wrong accounts without waiting for Christos to tell me.

I log into the system and try to pull up the first one on the list. But when I do, the password I've been given for it says *invalid*. I try again with the same result. As I make my way through the list, I'm denied over and over, and when I go to try the account I was working on only thirty minutes ago, I'm locked out of it too. I've had my access to every account I've ever touched cancelled.

All in the half hour since Christos visited my office.

**

Eventually Annais returns and I get a new set of accounts to work on. She seems as confused by the special codes as I was, but she says that she'll make sure to speak with Christos and find out which accounts she can safely assign to me and which she can't.

I'm finishing up for the day when I see a pretty brunette march by my desk, sniffling her way to Niko's office door where she throws it open and stomps on in, leaving it wide open behind her. I wonder if she's another of his scorned conquests, and though I know it's rude, I can't help but listen in.

"Cara," he says. "What are you doing here?"

Cara sobs and I hear Niko stand and go to her. "Aw, figgy, what's going on?

Was someone at school mean?"

I realize that this isn't one of Niko's conquests, but must be a sister or another cousin.

"No, Alex dumped me!" she cries.

I hear Niko comforting her while she sniffles.

"Figgy," he says, his voice gentle and warm. "You're getting snot all over my shirt. Now, come sit down and tell me what happened."

Little Cara pours out a story of woe that includes the asshole Alex deciding he'd rather take her friend Josie to the school dance. He's dumped her two days before the event, leaving her no time to get another date.

"First of all, I'll be talking to that little asshole's older brother, Dion. Trust me, Alex won't be doing something like that to another girl in this lifetime. Secondly, you have two choices—you can take Christos or me to the dance, or you can have a post-dance party on the yacht so you get to dress up and see all of your friends even without going. I'll chaperone and I'll ask Annais to also. That way Mom and Dad will be good with it."

"You'd do that for me?" she squeals in excitement.

"Of course I would. But you and your friends have to behave. No one trying to smoke or have sex on the boat, right?"

"I promise," she answers gravely. "I'll only invite the kids I trust. And my friends and I can decorate?"

"Yep. Do it up big time. I'll ask Constanza to cook some food for you too, just tell us how many kids you're going to invite."

I hear Cara squeal again and thank Niko, then she's skipping away down the hall past my desk, an entirely different person than when she came in. I look back at Niko's office and he's standing there watching her leave, a smile on his face.

"Younger sister?" I ask.

He strides over to my desk. "Yeah. You heard?" He doesn't seem offended by my eavesdropping so I cop to it.

"Yeah, sort of couldn't help it. Boy problems, huh?"

He nods. "Little shit. I want to kill him, but I know I probably did equally stupid things at his age."

I laugh. "Only at his age, huh?"

His gaze is heated when he looks back at me. "Maybe once or twice since then."

My breath hitches and I have to look away. I can't get caught up in fantasies about him. He's off-limits. Very, very off-limits.

"Well, you're a great big brother. You distracted her perfectly, and saved her social reputation in the bargain."

"Thanks," he answers. "Teenage girls are still kind of mysterious, but I know my sisters, and planning a party always makes them happy so I figured that was a safe idea."

"You did good." I smile at him and he beams back, obviously happy with the praise. "You remind me of my older brother, Nate. He's one of the good ones too. Some younger sisters get lucky."

He leans over, resting one palm on my desk. "Some friends do too," he murmurs before he turns and walks back to his office.

CHAPTER TWELVE

Niko

ForeignXChange Group

Darla: What the hell is an incidental? Like condoms?

I have to admit, she knew what she was doing. When Tess told me to come to a boat party with her friends from school, and bring nothing but a swimsuit, a towel and some cheap beer, it certainly didn't sound like a difficult assignment. Hell, a twelve year old should be able to manage all of that—with the substitution of soda for beer. It seemed easy—before I realized that the yacht was always stocked with towels, so I didn't actually know where we kept any, aside from the ones in my bathroom which the maid places there on a daily basis.

I spend the better part of an hour hunting through our villa, opening cabinets and closets, looking for something that resembles a beach towel like the ones we keep on board the yacht. I could grab a towel from the bathroom, but somehow I know I shouldn't. Maybe something my mother said to me as a kid sunk in. Finally, I'm forced to call Constanza at home, and she instructs me where to find them. In the pool house of course. Makes perfect sense now.

Once I've tossed on a t-shirt over my swim trunks, I get in the car and drive to the small neighborhood store not too far from my office. And that's where I'm standing, staring at the beer in the refrigerator section, astounded that I can get an entire six-pack of something for what one drink at a nightclub costs. Constanza buys all of our food for the house too, so I don't exactly visit the grocery store often.

I opt for Mythos and decide to get a case, not a six-pack. I'll probably get in trouble with Tess for it, but it would be really rude to show up without something to contribute to the group. Plus, Tess obviously doesn't know much about the drinking habits of a healthy twenty-four-year-old Greek guy. I could drink a six-pack of Mythos by myself in an afternoon on the water, and I wouldn't even be drunk.

I hop in my car and open the sunroof. It's a beautiful day on Georgios, and I'm more excited to go on this silly boat trip with a bunch of college kids than I've been in months, maybe longer. All the hours at nightclubs, the trips to Monaco to the casinos, the expensive bourbon and five hundred-dollar bottles of wine, the models and daughters of my dad's business colleagues, none of it was half as exciting to me as going on this little afternoon boat ride in waters that I know like the back of my hand, with cheap beer and a picnic lunch.

**

I arrive at the marina and hop out of the car, securing the case of beer and my towel under one arm. I haven't even made it to the rental shack yet when I hear Tess calling my name. I turn to see her and nearly lose all rational thought.

She's standing on the boardwalk with a couple of other girls, one of them the brunette who picked her up when she got off the ferry that first day. She's wearing some sort of cover-up thing like girls always wear, but it's transparent—white gauzy stuff that floats around her in the breeze and barely skims the tops of her thighs. Underneath is a tiny black bikini and a body that could make a grown man weep. I nearly do when my fucking conscience reminds me that I promised we'd be friends only. What the hell was I thinking?

She's got long golden legs, sweetly rounded hips, and smooth as cream tits that peek out tantalizingly from the small triangles of her bikini top. Her beautiful blonde hair is up in a messy bun of some sort, tendrils caressing her neck exactly where I'd like to put my lips.

"Hey," she says, as she gets closer. "You made it." She smiles at me and it's brighter than the Grecian sun. And so warm that something inside of my chest pinches painfully. I have to pause for a step to catch my breath.

"I wouldn't be anywhere else," I tell her, sounding like a lovelorn sap. I reach for the soft-sided cooler she's carrying on a shoulder strap. After looping it over my own shoulder I try to recover by being flippant. "My family's in shipping after all, boats are sort of my thing."

"And thank God for that," the brunette says. "Because I don't think any of the other guys know shit about boats."

I laugh and put out my hand. "I'm Niko."

She smirks at me. "Oh, yes you are." She shakes my hand. "Cass. The roommate."

Tess rolls her eyes. "You remember Cass from the day I got here, right?"

I nod and she turns to the other girl standing with them. "Una this is Niko, he—" she pauses and I tilt my head waiting to hear what she's going to say, "—he works with me. And Niko, this is Una, she's from Germany on exchange this year."

The German girl gives me the once over and then slips on a carnivorous smile.

"Nice to meet you," I say, decidedly disinterested even though she's hot. I may be here as Tess's friend only, but I'm not about to hit on someone else in front of her. I know enough about the confusing minds of women to realize that would be like signing my own death warrant.

Una's eyes narrow and she huffs out a breath before turning and flouncing off down the dock. Guess she got my message and didn't like it.

"I think they've got the boat about ready to go," Tess says, trying to cover the awkwardness. We all walk down the dock, toward a group of guys and girls standing next to the rental boats.

"I see you got twice as much beer as I told you to," she says. Cass tries to cover up a laugh, then she coughs while she blurts out "bossy".

"I brought some to share, but it's only Mythos. Definitely not fancy." I lean closer to her ear as we walk along. "How about my lunch? Did you bring me something good?" It sounds lascivious because it is. With her in that swimsuit my honorable intentions are being tested in the best possible way.

Somehow Cass heard me and turns as we get to the last boat in the slip. "We brought a ton of food, we've both got older brothers so we know the drill."

We all stop walking, and I finally look at the boat we're supposed to be spending the afternoon on. It's a standard waterskiing boat, built to hold ten people and it looks like there are nine of us ready to board it.

"This is going to be one crowded party," I mutter to myself.

"What?" Tess asks, giving me another one of those beautiful smiles. My more-than-friendly heart skips a beat.

I gaze at her, all semblance of casual speech blown out of my mind. Luckily, before I can steep more in humiliation with my stunned silence, a voice to my left says my name.

"Mr. Stephanos?" I turn and see an older man, Greek fishing cap perched on his head, his skin weathered and leathery. He's the walking cliché of the old Greek sailor.

"I had no idea this was your party," he exclaims in Greek. "You should have told me, I would have reserved something nicer for you."

I answer him in English so that I'm not rude to the rest of the group who are all watching us now. "This one is great. We're just going for a ride to catch some sun," I tell him, smiling as I shake his hand.

He's nervous as he nods his head up and down rapidly. "Maybe you'd rather take your ship?" He points down toward my dad's yacht sitting in dock at the end of the marina. It's twice the size of anything else here, and has the giant Stephanos logo on it, so it's not exactly inconspicuous.

"No," I tell the old man. "We're not taking the Stephanos ship today."

"That's yours, mate?" one of the guys in the group asks, jaw aflap.

I scratch the back of my head and dart a look at Tess, not sure how to handle this.

"My dad's actually," I say.

"Mr. Stephanos," the old sailor continues, still using Greek with me. "You need to go for a ride in your papa's ship today. This boat isn't good enough for you. We keep these for the tourists. You need something better."

This time I answer him in Greek, so that the others won't be able to understand. "Your boat is fine, really. I'm here as a guest. They're all students at the University and I don't want to make them uncomfortable with such a big ship. Do you understand what I mean?"

He nods. "Okay, if you say so, Mr. Stephanos. But if you're unhappy with this boat you come back and I'll try to find you something better."

I reassure the old guy that the rental boat is fine. Quoting an old Greek proverb to him that basically says to be mindful of what the group wants.

He smiles at me. "You're a fine man. Your papa is proud of you. Georgios is proud of you."

I thank him and he goes on to explain the little boat to us—to me really, since he seems to have forgotten that the guys who are actually renting it are there. When he finally leaves to go back to the rental shack we all board, get our stuff settled, and everyone introduces themselves.

"And you're Niko Stephanos," the British guy named Dominick says.

"I am," I answer.

"So all those monstrosities in the harbor belong to your family then?"

I laugh. "Yeah. They carry things like cars and railroad containers, they have to be big."

He nods.

I pull out a beer from the case I've stashed under one of the bench seats. "Brew?" I offer.

He nods, "Thanks, mate." I give his buddy another one and two of the girls take me up on them too. Everyone seems to settle in and Dominick takes the wheel, starting up the engine.

"You know how to drive one of these?" I ask.

"Nope, but I'm going to learn right now," he answers as we begin to move away from the dock.

Ten minutes and a couple of near misses later we've cleared the harbor and are comfortably out at sea, the shoreline still close by.

"I'm guessing you could drive this boat a lot better than Dominick," Tess whispers to me as the other girls gather in the seats at the bow of the boat, someone's iPod speakers blasting out dubstep and rap.

I smile at her and take a swig from my second beer. I quickly realized that only by slamming the first one would I relax enough to let good old Dominick steer us out of the marina without losing my shit.

"I come from a long line of sailors," I tell her. "I've been on boats and the water since I was old enough to walk, but I'm not sure what your rules are for this whole thing. I didn't want to come off as the pretentious rich guy taking over everything."

She shakes her head. "Okay, new rule. If it means saving our lives, you can be as pretentious as you want. Don't let us drown if you can pay for a helicopter to save us or something, all right?"

I chuckle. "Don't worry, princess, I won't let anything happen to you. Dominick can't pilot worth a damn, but these rental boats are nearly idiot proof and that sailboat he almost ran into was just screwing with us anyway. It was Darvos Andrade and he can sail a boat through the eye of a needle, so he would have never let us get that close unless he wanted to scare the crap out of you all."

"That's just mean," she says, but her eyes are laughing and her lips twitch. God, I'd like to wipe that smirk off of her face, replace it with ecstasy.

I lean back and get as comfortable as I can on the fake leather seats of the little boat. Dominick has cut the engine now and we're drifting, one of the guys has dived into the water and the girls have all shed their cover-ups.

"What was the old guy at the marina saying to you?" she asks, cocking her head to one side like a cute little puppy.

I clear my throat, not sure why this makes me uncomfortable, but it does.

"He thought maybe I'd prefer to go out on my family's boat."

"Ah." She nods. "You've probably never been on one of these little rentals, huh?"

I shrug. "I don't really recall, but if it gets you out on the water it's all good."

She looks back toward the harbor where my dad's yacht sits. "I guess the whole idea of you being an average person is pretty far fetched no matter how cheap the beer you're drinking."

I shake my head. "Believe it or not, even though I'm spoiled and out of touch, I sometimes wish I was average."

She looks at me thoughtfully for a moment, her sunglasses obscuring what I might learn from her eyes.

"No matter how much money you might or might not have, you could never be average," she tells me, her raw honesty digging deep into my chest, puncturing places I didn't even know were there.

I clear my throat, slightly overcome by her beauty, not just her looks.

"Careful, princess," I say, my voice rough. "I promised I'd be your friend, but you'll get my hopes up for more if you keep sweet talking me like that."

She laughs softly. "Are you hungry?"

"I'm a guy, I'm always hungry."

"Good, I made you something from home—Illinois, I mean. Let me go get it."

She scoots up to the front of the boat where the coolers and all the other people are. I pin my eyes to the horizon, in an effort not to look at her ass in that bikini.

"That was sweet," Cass says as she sits next to me in the spot vacated by Tess. "What you told the old man at the marina. How you didn't want to horn in on the plans these guys had already made."

"You speak Greek." Somehow I'm not surprised. Cass speaks very American English, but something about her is familiar, like looking at photos of a place you've vacationed in multiple times.

"My mom's from here. My dad's American," she answers. It all makes perfect sense.

"Tess is trying to train the billionaire out of me." I laugh. "Think she can do it?"

"Why would you want her to?"

"Apparently I can be somewhat of an ass," I say.

"Yeah, the guy who wanted to spare the feelings of a bunch of college kids is a real ass. Also the guy who's slumming it to make his intern at work happy." She looks at me skeptically. "But that's right, you've got the hots for her, so you'll do about anything to get in her pants I bet."

I feel my face heat. I'm not sure if I'm pissed that she's implying I'm being dishonest, or embarrassed that she can tell how badly I have it for Tess.

"Tess is great, but I'm not doing this for any reason other than I think she's right. I can be an entitled jerk a lot of the time, and worse, I don't even realize it usually."

I pause, wondering how much I should tell a girl I barely know. "Tess is the perfect person to help me with that because she's not from here. Let's just say that most of the people I'm around every day would never even think to tell me I'm being an ass."

"Huh." She squints at me.

"What?" I ask. This girl makes me nervous, like she's going to hex me or something.

"You really don't see it?"

"See what?"

"The fact that you're letting little Tess Richardson from Illinois, USA tell you how to act is proof that you're *not* a rich dick. But even more than that it's proof that you like her an awful lot."

"It's not like that," I say, looking at her sharply.

"Riiight," she answers.

Tess comes back then, and interrupts us with a cooler full of ham and cheese sandwiches along with orange sodas and salt and vinegar potato chips. It's about as regular as you can get, and I love every bite.

CHAPTER THIRTEEN

Tess

ForeignXChange Group

Tess: Foster, have you had the fish and chips yet? I can't stop thinking about them now.

The nation of Greece has not fully exploited their greatest natural resource—the bare chest of Niko Stephanos.

When he whipped off his shirt after lunch and dove into the water I nearly swooned right on the deck of our little floating party palace. And to top off the tan skin, cut abs, hard as steel pecs, and treasure trail that is begging me to touch, he's being the perfect guest. He made friends with the guys from Britain, even subtly giving Dominick a few pointers on piloting the boat. He charmed Cass to the point that she leaned over and whispered in my ear, "If you don't do him, I will." He had Una and Cristal laughing so hard over some joke about the Eurozone economy that Una forgot to be offended he wasn't hitting on her.

Now he's treading water a few feet away as I sit on the back of the boat with my legs dangling into the water.

"Come on," he pleads. "Just hop in, it's great out here."

I shake my head. "Huh, uh. I swim in lakes, not the ocean. There are all sorts of…things…in that water."

He laughs and slicks back his wet hair, exposing those crystal blue eyes even more.

"What kinds of things are you talking about?"

"Sharks," I shout at him. "There are sharks in oceans and I saw Jaws when I was eight and I've been scared to swim in the ocean ever since." There. I said it.

He stares at me for a moment, then swims over, placing a hand around one of my ankles. He looks up at me earnestly. "Really? You're scared of sharks?"

I nod, knowing I'm completely pathetic.

"Well," he says softly, placing his other hand around my other ankle. "You don't need to be." He strokes his hands up and down my ankles and calves, and I nearly forget to breathe. Tingles shoot up and down my legs, and I sigh with pleasure as his thumbs massage the sensitive skin around my heels.

"There's nothing to be afraid of out here, princess." His voice is hypnotic, soft, gritty, sexy as hell. "Because the only shark in Greece…is me!" He jerks my ankles hard, and I slide right off the slick plastic of the boat before I fly over the water for a split second then land with a crash, dipping under before Niko lifts me up by my elbows, holding me close as I splutter and shake the water out of my face.

"Oh my God!" I shriek. "You did not do that!"

He chuckles as we tread water, facing one another. I can see the drops of water sparkling on his long, dark eyelashes. They're like tiny diamonds.

"I did do that," he says. "And you're going to thank me for helping you overcome your fear. The last time there was a shark attack in Greek waters was the middle ages or something. You're more likely to run into a hydra than a shark."

"A hydra?" I look around frantically at the surface of the water. "What the hell is that? Oh my God. Let me back on the boat."

I struggle to get out of his grasp, but he pulls me into his chest, wrapping his arms around my shoulders. "Shhh," he soothes, his mouth next to my ear. "Calm down, princess. A hydra's a mythological creature—a kraken, you know? There are no hydras, no sharks, just you and me, and the deep blue sea."

He's using the voice again, and I relax, holding still in his arms, feeling the sun on my wet hair, the water caressing my skin. I inhale and smell salt, and sea, and something citrusy from Niko's hair. My heart beats double-time, and I realize that I'm in so much trouble. This guy—this billionaire—is like a hero in a movie. As much as I've tried to turn him into a villain, he's not. He's a hero—warm, funny, considerate, gorgeous, sexy.

I don't know that I ever really thought he'd fire me if we had a fling that didn't go well. I think I convinced myself of it to push him away, because the fact is that

I'm afraid. Afraid to get close to him, afraid to like him too much. Afraid to want something I know I can't have. In my life I've only ever gone after the possible. I'm not afraid of hard work, but I know the rules. I know what things I'm allowed and what things I'm not. I stick to those—the practical, the doable, the attainable. And for someone like me, Niko Stephanos is absolutely not one of those things. He's a Greek billionaire. I'm a cop's daughter from Illinois. There may not be an actual rule against us, but there's surely an unwritten one.

Self-preservation kicks in and I slide out of Niko's hold like a water snake, propelling myself away from the boat, and kicking up water that hits him in the face. "You may have hydras here," I call over my shoulder. "But we have the Lake Michigan Monster, and I can outswim him. Get a move on Greek boy." I take off, swimming my hardest, and it isn't long before I feel Niko by my side, racing me to nowhere, in the golden Grecian sun. I try not to think that I might be breaking the biggest rule of them all—losing my heart to a guy I can never have.

**

"Niko's not at all like you said," Cass tells me as we lounge in front of a movie later that night.

"Oh yeah? In what way?"

"Well, he's not an arrogant jerk for one thing."

I wiggle around, trying to get comfortable on the second-hand sofa that's some kind of crushed velvet and scratchy as hell.

"Trust me, he can be. But yeah, he's not always."

"He likes you."

Cass is ever-blunt, and I feel my cheeks heat.

"We're just friends. You know that's the deal."

"But it doesn't change the fact that he likes you. As more than a friend."

I turn the volume up on the movie. Then back down. Then up again.

"Teh-ehs," she says in a singsong voice.

"What?" I squirm some more.

"Are you going to ignore it forever. Hang out together and never admit that you both have huge crushes?"

"What do you want me to say, Cass? Our crushes don't matter—they can't matter. I need the job, he understands that. His dad even said he doesn't want him dating the staff. We'd both get in trouble."

She sniffs and looks at the television for a few minutes. "You guys just seem really cute—"

"Stop!" I laugh, throwing a pillow at her head. "We would be really cute, but we can't, so just stop. It's hard enough as it is."

"Okay, okay. But for the record, I think you're nuts."

"For the record, I do too," I mumble, tucking my feet up under me and laying my head down on the arm of the sofa. "Certifiable."

**

Later that night while I'm in bed reading for my economics course, my phone chimes. I pick it up off the nightstand and look at the glowing screen.

Niko: Thought you'd like to know that Cara's party is a success.

He's attached a picture of his little sister in front of an elaborately decorated table full of food and fancy, iced cakes. She has her arms slung around two other girls, and all three of them are in formal dresses. Lanterns and streamers hang from the ceiling behind them.

Me: Look how pretty! You're such a good big brother. No teens trying to get it on in the bunks or whatever you have on a yacht?

Niko: I busted up a couple of boys trying to light a doobie out on deck, but no sex so far.

Me: Kids these days. We would have totally snuck into the bedrooms.

Niko: Oh yeah? And what would teenage Tess have done with the boys in a dark bedroom at a party?

My heart beats with excitement, imagining Niko and I in a room like that, the fear of getting caught making everything seem so much more urgent.

Me: Depends on who I was with.

The response is slow to come, and I think that maybe he's gotten distracted, or knows we're treading in dangerous territory, but then the phone chimes again and I'm almost afraid to look.

Niko: Maybe it was a teenage Niko.

My lungs constrict. I can imagine all too well the kinds of things teenage Tess would have done with teenage Niko. I think about my response for a long while, reminding myself that we are supposed to be friends. And while friends can flirt a bit here and there, I shouldn't let this go too far. No matter how much I'd like to.

Me: I think teenage Tess would have been tempted to do most anything with teenage Niko.

His response is immediate.

Niko: But is grown up Tess tempted by the same things?

I gasp, heat flowing through me, my core tingling in response to the thoughts that invade my mind. His body and mine, sliding, slick, hot, writhing. Tongues and fingers, silk and steel.

Before I can answer he texts again.

Niko: Sorry. That was out of line. Please forgive me.

I shake my head trying to dispel the lust that's taken over my rational side.

Me: Nothing to forgive. My fault too. I'm glad your sister's having a good time. I'll see you on Monday.

Niko: Thanks again for the boat party. I had a great time.

Me: You're welcome. I had fun too.

Niko: Good night, Tess. Sweet dreams.

Me: Good night.

CHAPTER FOURTEEN

Niko

ForeignXChange Group

Kellie: I had fish and chips! They were really good, but I have to be careful about what I eat. I'm in training until the World Feis is over. But, I met someone, his name is Aiden, and I'll break the training rules for him anytime.

Touching Tess.

It's all I can think about. I remember the feel of her slick skin under my hands as I held her in the ocean. I remember the scent of her hair as I lowered my head to her shoulder in the nightclub. I remember the warmth of her gaze as I clutched her hand on the table at lunch. My mind is overrun with thoughts of touching Tess.

Which might explain why I'm late to work on Monday morning and my father is sitting in my office waiting for me.

"Pop," I say as I enter the room and set my laptop bag down. "You're here early."

He gives me a kiss on each cheek before gently cuffing me upside the head. "I'm not early, you're late."

"Yeah, sorry. You can ask Annais, I'm normally here before this. I didn't sleep well last night."

He makes a motion with his hand as if brushing away the issue of my tardiness. "Eh, you didn't sleep well because you didn't come to church or Sunday dinner like your mother asked."

Shit. I should have known skipping both was likely to bring down the wrath of Ari.

"Okay, okay. I'll make sure to come to both next week, how's that?"

I take a seat behind my desk while my dad continues to walk around the room looking at things on my walls—my diploma, photos of me playing soccer at Miami, an article about me that was in the Athens newspaper last year when I came to work full-time for the company.

"You haven't talked to me about work lately," he states, with no segue.

I shrug. "Nothing much to talk about. Everything's running like it should be. No one seems to have any big complaints—at least not that I've heard." I look at him, wondering if something's gone wrong that I don't know about. He wanders back to my desk and finally sits down in one of the chairs facing me.

"I hear nothing but good things," he says, and I feel that rush of breath that happens when you've been holding it without realizing you were.

"Well, we aim to please here in Finance," I joke.

He shifts in his chair and watches me for a moment. As rough as he might appear, and as well-known as he is for being hard-nosed in the business world, my dad has never been anything but gentle and loving with my sisters and me. He's like a big, gruff teddy bear. The only time he's ever raised his voice in our house was when I was a teen home from boarding school for the summer, a little too full of myself and my own importance. I made my mother cry when I stayed out all night with Christos and some girls we met at the beach that day. My father called me into his office at the house the next morning after I wandered in hungover, having spent most of the night banging Athena Papadous.

My sisters told me later that they could hear Dad yelling clear out at the pool, his deep voice booming throughout the property as he told me that he didn't care how old I got, how big I got, how many women I screwed, or how much money I earned, if I ever made my mother cry again he'd kick my ass across the island and disown me to boot.

Needless to say he scared the crap out of me, and I never tested my mother's rules again.

"I heard that you went down to the docks the other day," he says, almost too nonchalantly.

I think for a moment. "Oh, yeah. I saw some of our guys loading these weird crates onto a tanker. I couldn't figure out what kind of cargo it might be, didn't look like anything that we'd normally put on a tanker so I thought I'd check up on it."

He nods, thoughtfully. "And what did they tell you?"

"It was medical supplies they said. But they were going from LA to Syria. Why would they stop and unload and reload that stuff here? Isn't that odd to you? I'm worried that someone might be padding shipping costs and skimming the difference." I lean my elbows on my desk, thinking how strange it is to have him sitting in front of the desk and me behind it, and I can't help but wonder why one simple visit to the docks has brought my father here from his CEO suite first thing in the morning.

His blue eyes look tired, and for the first time that I can recall, he looks his age, the fifty-one years of life displayed in his skin, his graying temples, and his worn posture. My heart skips a beat and for a moment the idea that he might be ill flashes through my mind. It scares me, more than I'd ever admit to another human being. My father is my anchor, the thing in this world that keeps me grounded. It doesn't matter if I see him every day or once a year, if he's down the block or thousands of miles away, he's the touchstone that I use to remember who I am, what I have, and how incredibly fortunate I am in this life. He's my role model in all things. A brilliant businessman, a kind and generous boss, a loyal husband, and loving father—I'm not sure I could live in a world that doesn't include my dad.

"I'm proud of you," he says softly. "It makes my heart warm to know that you love this company as much as I do, as your grandfather did. You notice the small things, and you care enough to ask about them.

That's the mark of a leader. You'll lead this company to even greater things than I have."

I smile, warming under his praise, which he doesn't give unless he genuinely believes it.

"But a great CEO cannot spend his time dealing with those little things," he continues. "You need to learn to delegate more, this is why I have people working for you. And believe me, it will go much better for someone on your staff to go down to the docks and ask the questions than for you to do it."

I hadn't thought about that. When I showed up did it scare them? Make them nervous? I didn't mean it to. Once again though it sounds like Tess is right about me—I don't very often put myself in the shoes of others.

"I'm sorry, Pop. I didn't think about how it might come off to the staff. I'm not used to thinking that the boss is scary to a lot of people."

He gives me a tight smile. "It's okay. You're learning every day. Now you know, so next time you have a concern like that you just take it to Christos, he'll handle it for you, that's his job. You let him talk to the staff, you have other things to do with your time."

I know he's trying to help, and I realize that he's right about the front line staff being a little uncomfortable with me in their business, but I also can't help but feel a sliver of something unpleasant. Like the possibility that my father trusts Christos more than he trusts me. Given some of the things Christos has said to me recently I'm not sure he warrants it. Then there's the possibility that I'm so protected and coddled and surrounded by family all the time not because I'm the heir, but because my father doesn't view me as capable.

I swallow the bitterness. "Whatever you say, Pop. I'll let Christos handle things like that from now on."

He nods and smiles, looking ten times more relaxed than when he came in. "That's my boy," he stands. I do as well and walk around the edge of the desk to his side. "You bring this face home to your mother next Sunday, yeah?" He pinches my cheeks before giving one a light tap.

"Yeah. I will," I answer.

"Good. I'll see you on Sunday." He pulls his phone out of his jacket pocket and looks at the screen, swiping it to rearrange whatever he's seeing. He glances up, distracted. "I'll tell Mama you're coming to church, she'll be happy all week."

"All right, see you then."

After he's exited my office, I'm left with the lingering odor of Polo cologne, and the lingering realization that my father didn't even flinch at the possibility that someone might be stealing from his company.

**

After my dad's visit, Monday and Tuesday at the office fly by. We've got several new accounts, and our Middle Eastern fleet is undergoing annual maintenance, so there's a lot of shuffling of schedules and shipments that has to occur to accommodate the new customers.

Wednesday I finally get a chance to catch up on my regular paperwork, signing off on invoices, answering emails, and tying up loose ends on some of the reports staff have been preparing for the quarterly audits.

It's past eight p.m. when I finally throw my pen down on my desk and take a moment to rest my tired eyes. I've been sitting in one spot for hours, and I realize that I'm hungry, thirsty, and stiff. I stand and stretch before deciding to wander to the kitchenette down the hall and make myself some coffee.

There's a desk lamp light on at Tess's desk, and I assume she or one of the maintenance people left it on. I go through the reception area and am headed to the kitchen when I hear the copy machine running and notice the light shining from under the door of the printer room. I rap on the door twice before turning the knob and sticking my head in, hoping that Annais isn't here this late. Her husband will never forgive me for keeping her here through dinner.

I'm greeted by the sight of Tess bending over the copier loading more paper into the industrial-sized tray at the bottom of the machine. She's wearing a pair of those shorts that women wear to the office, they come to mid-thigh, and they're tailored like men's dress pants, but they're white, and she has a deep red t-shirt in some sort of silky material on with them. Her shoes are red also, and have a high platform heel. Tess always wears super high heels to work, and I know it's because she's self-conscious about being short, but I won't complain because they make her legs look so fucking sexy it takes my breath away.

I stare at her ass for a moment as she works to get the paper in the drawer of the copier. She might be small, but she's got a perfect ass—round, firm, and begging for me to take a bite out of it like a juicy apple. She stands and I can't help but grin at the image.

"Knock knock," I finally say, knowing I can't be a creeper anymore without her catching me.

She whirls around, her hand at her throat. "Oh! God, you startled me. I didn't realize anyone else was here."

"Sorry. I didn't know you were here either. Are we giving you too much work?"

She punches the button to start the copier up again, and smiles. If I didn't know better, I'd swear the sun had leaked into this windowless room.

"Not at all. I needed the presentation software you have here for some schoolwork, then I decided to take care of this copying Annais wants for a meeting tomorrow morning so I wouldn't have to come in early."

"The school doesn't give you the apps you need?" I ask, thinking that we should buy her whatever she needs so she can do her schoolwork at home like a normal college student.

"No. I think it's a really common program here in Europe, but we don't use it in the States. I'm sure they figure everyone has it." Her face suddenly falls. "Oh my gosh, should I not be using the company computers for homework? I am so sorry, I had no idea." Her cheeks turn pink and she clenches her hands together. "I asked Annais and she said it was fine, but I didn't even think that I should check with you. Oh my God, I can't believe this—"

I stride to her in one large step and capture her wringing hands in mine. "Shh, princess. It's okay, you didn't do anything wrong."

She stops, her breath hitching a little as her eyes search mine. "I didn't?"

I can't help but chuckle. My poor little rule follower. "Not at all. You're our intern, you're here to learn—from us, from school, from living in a different country. When we take on an intern we do it because we want to support their education, that includes letting you use the company equipment."

She sighs in relief, gently pulling her hands from mine, which causes my heart to squeeze like a sponge that's being wrung out. Suddenly everything inside of me feels dry and desolate.

"In fact," I continue, "I want you to have the programs you need at home. Bring your laptop in to the IT guys and have them load anything you need on it so that you don't have to stay late here."

"Seriously?" Her eyes are lighted up and all I can think is that I'd give her the whole damn company if she'd look at me like this every day.

"Yes, for sure."

"There's not a rule against that is there? I mean, you won't get in trouble for giving me something you don't give everyone else?"

I shake my head. She still doesn't get it. "Princess, I've got an IT budget that I can do whatever I want with. Including give my staff the tools they need to do work outside of the office. Lots of staff have company software loaded on their laptops that they use at home."

"Okay. Oh, that's good. Wow, and thank you so much. I can't believe how generous that is."

I lean back against the counter across from the copier and stuff my hands in my pockets so that I won't reach for her. Gratitude is a good look on Tess. I'd like to do all sorts of things to earn her gratitude, starting with my mouth on hers and ending with my mouth somewhere much lower. I shift, trying to stem the rising tide in my dress pants. Time to shift gears.

"Have you had dinner?" I ask.

"No. I was hoping that Cass left something in the fridge at home. She usually stays at her boyfriend's on Wednesdays, but she also cooks a lot and leaves me the leftovers."

"Come with me," I tell her as I reach over to the copier and collect her stack of papers. "We'll drop these off on the way."

A few minutes later we're in the office kitchen, an odd assortment of items spread out on the counter.

"Olives, rice pilaf, tangerines, and some sort of bacon bits." Tess surveys the mish mash of food. "You think we can make a dinner out of this?"

"Sure," I say, sounding a lot more confident than I am. "Watch." I take the rice pilaf and toss the bacon bits on top of it, then the olives before I put it in the microwave and hit the minute heat button. Then I open the refrigerator again and dig around until I come up with a jar of tzatziki sauce. Tess watches me with an amused look on her face, obviously committed to letting me make a botched mess of this whole thing.

The microwave dings and I pull out the rice, bacon, olive mess, drizzle the tzatziki sauce over the top, then slice the tangerine in half, putting each half on small plates before scooping the rice mixture onto the plates as well.

I put the plates on the table we keep for staff to eat lunch at, then I bow deeply. "Your dinner is served mademoiselle."

Tess giggles, and shakes her head. "No way."

"What?" I ask, grinning. "It's got a meat, a vegetable, a grain, a fruit and the tzatziki sauce is dairy. All the food groups."

I pull out a chair and gesture for her to sit. After she's seated I take the other chair and pick up my fork. "You going to chicken out on me?" I ask, knowing that Tess has a competitive streak.

Her brows pinch and she growls, "Oh, hell no."

I laugh and watch as she lifts a forkful up, looking at it skeptically before she shoves it in her mouth and chews tentatively.

Her eyes grow rounder and she points at me with her fork. I lift mine and dig in, taking a big bite and chewing with gusto. "It's really not that bad," she says around the mouthful of food. "Right?"

I chew a couple of more times, then swallow. "Tolerable," I answer. "I'm not convinced that tzatziki and bacon were meant to be friends, but other than that it's fine."

She laughs, and we settle in to our strange meal. She's easy to talk to and I find myself telling her about my days playing soccer, hearing about her two state medals in high school swimming—not a surprise, having raced her at the party over the weekend and nearly lost. The only reason I was able to pull it off is that she was a fifty and one hundred-meter specialist, the shortest distances. She can beat me at those sprints, but in open water my endurance won out.

I've been telling her about the conference championship we won in college, detailing how Christos was stupid enough to show up to the semi-finals hungover. Instead of worrying about nixing our chances at the cup, our coach wanted to punish Christos, so he made him play the entire game.

"Christos was puking on the sidelines every time there was a throw-in, and the ref even had a talk with our coach about pulling him out, but coach refused." I chuckle remembering that Christos was actually a pale shade of green when halftime came.

"Can I ask you something?"

"Sure," I answer, standing and throwing both of our paper plates away. "You want to come to my office? I've got a bottle of wine in my desk drawer and the sofa is a hell of a lot more comfortable than these plastic chairs."

She looks unsure but it's only for a moment, then she agrees. It warms me all over that I've gained her trust enough she'll sit with me in my office alone after hours.

When we get there, I pour her a small glass of merlot when we settle on the sofa, me at one end, turned to watch her. She's got her feet up on my coffee table, and I resist the urge to pick up her legs and put them on my lap so I can rub those pretty toes.

"What did you want to know?" I ask once we're both comfortable.

"Something kind of strange happened last week and I'm probably showing how inexperienced I am, but I've been confused ever since."

I can tell she's nervous to talk to me about it, but I don't want Tess to ever be nervous with me again. I give her my most encouraging smile. "It's okay. Like I said before, you're an intern, you're here to learn. There aren't any dumb questions. Not with me."

She returns my smile with a shy one of her own and as girly as it sounds, things flutter inside my chest. I try to brush it off and focus on what she has to say, even though that means looking at her soft pink lips and big blue eyes. I'm drowning, and while I'm an expert in the water, I can't seem to save myself from this.

I continue to focus on listening as Tess tells me a story about the accounts she was assigned when she started work, and how there were mystery codes associated with them. She struggled to figure them out, asking various staff members here and in the Athens office, but it was Christos who finally told her they were some of our *special* accounts. My whole body tenses when she says the word—special. We don't have special accounts at Stephanos. We don't have special codes. We handle all of our accounts the same way. We have for as long as I've been working at the company— since I was fifteen and had my first summer job at the docks, loading and unloading the ships that Dad keeps in port here.

Christos lied to Tess. The only question is, why?

As much as I want to, I can't out my oldest, dearest friend, my own blood, to Tess, a girl I've known for a few weeks. So I act as though these special accounts are the norm, and tell her to continue with the story.

She takes a deep breath. "Afterwards, I wanted to go through the other accounts I had to see if they had those codes. I realized that I'd given all of my work to Christos and I didn't want to sit around for the next four hours with nothing to do. But when I went to open up the rest of the accounts all of my passwords were invalid."

I look at her for a moment, trying to process what she's saying.

"It was a half hour after I told Christos about those codes, and in that thirty minutes I'd been locked out of every one of the accounts."

The feeling of unease that began when she said Christos had special accounts magnifies now. It's pretty obvious that Christos immediately locked her out of those accounts. What isn't clear is why. Did he think she'd do something wrong with them? That's sort of impossible though since all of the raw data about our accounts is unalterable. The books are the books, you can't mess them up. All that Tess was doing is preparing reports based on that data. Something is very wrong, and my gut tells me I'm not going to like what I hear from Christos, but I can't answer Tess's concerns until I speak with him.

"You know," I say, hating myself for lying, feeling the words come out of me like bile that I want to shove back down. "I think Christos may have a habit of putting new passwords on all of the accounts that come across his desk. Just so he can control who's got access to them. He once got in trouble for a mistake that someone in the bookkeeping section had made. He's sort of paranoid now." I try to laugh it off, but my voice sounds hollow even to my own ears.

She watches me for a minute, her face neutral. I scramble to fix it.

"I'll ask him though if it would make you feel better?"

She nods. "It would. I'm sorry, I'm not trying to be trouble. But I'm worried I did something I shouldn't have and Christos didn't want to reprimand me so he just locked me out instead." She's so earnest it breaks my heart. "But I need to know if I've made mistakes. No babying me, I need to know straight up. It's the only way I'll learn."

My heart swells with admiration again for this beautiful woman with her ethics and her rules and her bravery. She's so different than anyone I've ever known, and it amazes me how much I crave it. I crave her views, her drive, her steely determination. I love trying to support her in following the rules as much as I do trying to nudge her away from them. It's a game that I could play forever—convince Tess to break a rule, then follow one to please her.

I've just promised to question Christos—that's following a rule to please her. Now it's time to see if I can get her to break one in return.

"You ever been to the water at night?" I ask as I grab the wine bottle off the coffee table in front of me.

She shakes her head, her expression suspicious.

"You trust me?" I ask.

She swallows, and I watch the motion, my whole body aching with the need that it drives through me. The need to run my tongue along that path up her neck, to her lips, inside her warm, wet mouth. My breath hitches and I clear my throat.

"Tess?" I ask softly.

"Yes," she answers, her voice rougher than usual, her eyes dilated. "I trust you."

I take her hand gently in mine. "Then let me show you something."

CHAPTER FIFTEEN

Tess

ForeignXChange Group

Tess: Foster, I think it might be time for you to tell me that story about you sleeping with your boss...

I'm following Niko across the street toward the boardwalk along the harbor, and while I know I shouldn't be doing this, I can't stop myself. His hand is big and warm, and the air around us is fresh and salty. In the humid stillness the lights of a handful of boats out on the dark water are like stars in the vast inkiness of a night sky.

Neither of us speaks until we've reached the marina a couple of blocks away from the Stephanos offices.

"You okay?" he asks quietly.

"Yeah. But curious. Where are we going?"

He turns to look at me, and I'm breathless for a moment from his beauty. He's wearing a white button down shirt open more than normal at the throat, his dark skin displayed to perfection in the V of the neckline. The sleeves are rolled midway up his forearms, and he's wearing a big bulky watch on his left wrist. It's metal, with all sorts of dials and gauges on it—expensive, substantive, complex—a reminder that he's so much more than a twenty-something guy taking a walk with a girl. He's wealthy, powerful, favored in every way.

He smiles, unaware that my hormones and my common sense are at war.

"We're almost there," he says as we turn to walk along one of the docks that jut out into the water of the harbor.

We walk on the dock as it shifts subtly from side to side, the water slapping against the wood underneath us. We're midway to the end when he suddenly stops, turning to a boat looming in the shadows thrown by the moonlight.

"Come on," he says, pulling me toward the railing along the deck of the ship.

"Wait, what are we doing?" I ask, resisting for the first time since we left the office.

"It's okay," he says softly, leaning into my ear, his breath sending a frisson of awareness down my neck and shoulder. "It's mine."

I look more carefully at the boat. It's big. Not big like a yacht, but big enough that it has a cabin underneath the deck. I can make out a mast of some sort in the gloom, so it must be a sailboat. I've seen the occasional high-end sailboat out on Lake Michigan, but mostly we have boats for waterskiing there. Big motorboats that you pile people and equipment on for a day's worth of sports and partying. There's something much more classical about this boat. It's like old family money next to the nouveau riche.

"This is yours?"

He chuckles. "It is."

Then, before I know what's happening he puts his hands on my waist and swings me up and over the railing onto the deck. I gasp, both at the sensation of flying and the feeling of his hands cradling me so strong and commanding. Once I'm safely on board he grasps the railing with both hands and pushes himself up before swinging his legs over and landing next to me, graceful as a cat.

"Welcome aboard," he says with a grin so wide I can feel it as much as see it.

"So this is a sailboat?" I ask as I start to walk along the railing, trailing my hand on the cool metal and looking at the smooth deck under my feet.

"It is. A thirty-two-foot day cruiser."

"You realize that means nothing to me," I tell him.

He laughs. "It means that I can sail it by myself, and if I have to I can even sleep on it, but it's not set up for long trips out at sea."

"That's what you have the yacht for." I can't believe I'm having a discussion about yachts as if it's normal conversation.

He takes my hand and moves us around the small deck to a built-in bench along the back end. We sit and he leans back, relaxing into the seat and gazing up at the sky.

"You want to know the truth?" he asks, not looking at me.

"Always," I answer, watching the way his thick hair shines in the moonlight, and crossing my arms so I won't reach out to touch the silky strands.

"The yacht is nice and all, but it really doesn't interest me that much." He finally turns and looks at me, his expression is pensive, almost as if he's worried I'll think less of him after this confession. "It's great for parties and all that, but you could be on a bus or a plane, or sitting around at your house when you're on that thing. There's no—" He pauses. "No sense that you're on the water. No connection, you know?"

I nod my head, wanting him to go on, feeling as though this is the closest I've gotten to a glimpse of the real Niko, the soft inside of such a flawless exterior.

"I love the water. I have since the first time my dad took me out on a little dinghy he filched from the yacht one afternoon while we were cruising.

"But for me, it's about *feeling* the water, not just touching it, but feeling it inside me. When I'm sailing and it's going right—the boat, the wind, me, the ocean—we're all working together in tandem. I'm part of something bigger than me, bigger than human beings or any of our constructs. I'm part of this wild, unstoppable thing that's allowing me to work with it, and it could change its mind at any moment."

He sighs, then chuckles. "Annd now the pretty girl thinks I'm nuts," he jokes self-deprecatingly.

I put my hand on his arm and hear his sharp intake of breath. My voice is husky, and we're both almost whispering in the quiet of the night.

"I don't think you're crazy, Niko. I think you're smart and committed and kind of amazing sometimes. It's inspiring that you have that connection with the water. I don't think I've ever felt like that about anything."

His eyes are so dark they're nearly black, and his face is a relief in shadows thrown by the lights of the dock and the moon and the stars. He clears his throat and gently asks, "But I'm still also selfish and insensitive?"

"No." I shake my head in conjunction with my response. My heart feels heavy inside my body, and I long to melt against him, lay my head on his shoulder, and pretend that we're two people who could actually fall in love with one another. "I was wrong when I said those things. You're incredibly generous, and more real than half the starving college students I know."

We sit in silence, each stuck in our own thoughts, but I'm so aware of him. My skin tingles, and I hear every breath he takes, every smallest shift of his muscles.

"Stay right here," he finally says, standing and disappearing down the stairs to the cabin. When he returns he's got another bottle of wine and a blanket with him. He spreads the blanket out on the deck and uncorks the wine that he must have opened below.

"Come on," he tells me, pointing to the blanket. He sits down on it, and takes a swig out of the wine bottle.

I join him, unable to help the smile that creases my cheeks. I think of how many women would give an arm or a leg to be on a sailboat in Greece with a super hot billionaire and a bottle of wine. When did my life become a romance novel?

"I didn't have any glasses. Hope you don't mind sharing the bottle even though it's against hygiene rules or whatever." He smirks, daring me to turn it down.

I roll my eyes. "There are some rules I'm willing to break." I take the bottle and swallow a warm, spicy mouthful of the dark, fruity table wine.

Niko lies down on his back, one arm across his stomach and the other bent under his head. "You know most of these stars were named by the ancient people right here in these islands," he tells me.

I take another swig of the wine before I set the bottle aside and lie next to him, staring up at the dense blanket of lights, so much brighter here than in Chicago with its big city light pollution.

"My dad used to read me this book that had all the constellations in it. It told all the myths that went with the constellations. I loved the Greek myths," I tell him.

"Sometimes," he answers, "when I'm sailing around the island, taking it easy on a low wind day, I try to wrap my head around the fact that human beings have been on ships sailing these waters, watching these same views for tens of thousands of years. I wonder what they thought about, what their boats looked like, who their families were."

I turn to my side and look at his profile. The firm jawline, the straight nose and long eyelashes. My heart flutters and I swallow, my throat suddenly dry.

"Some of them were probably your great times twenty grandparents," I say.

He turns his head to look at me and smiles, then rolls onto his side to face me. We're inches apart, our breath mingling in the night air.

"Yes. I think about that too. When I was in boarding school and college I came to realize how unusual it is to live in the place where your family has been for thousands of years. To know when you walk around each day that your great, great, great grandparents walked along these same roads, stared at this same slice of sky, touched these same grains of sand."

My breath catches and my heart races as I feel his hand tentatively touch mine where it rests in between our bodies. I don't move, and he gently clasps my fingertips. It's such a sweet gesture that I melt into the deck of his ship, becoming a puddle of warm sensations, girlish fantasies and molten desire.

"I can't imagine having a history like that. I barely know where my grandparents grew up, much less an ancestor who's four or five generations back."

He sighs, and his eyes blink shut for a brief moment. "I love it. I love Greece…" He pauses. "But I'm not sure if I love it enough."

"What does that mean?" I wait for his answer, almost afraid to breathe.

He huffs out a sharp chuckle. "I've never told anyone this before." He shakes his head as though he can't believe he's about to admit this to me, then he looks at me and all the pretense is gone, all that's left is raw honesty, and somewhere in his eyes a plea for understanding.

"The whole heir thing—being the prince of Stephanos—I don't always love it. I don't always love the company or working there."

"Oh," I say, since it's the only thing I can think of.

"Don't get me wrong, I realize how fortunate I am, and of course I like the things—cars, houses, trips. This boat." He grins. "But the longer I've been out of school…" He struggles seeming to search for the perfect word, then gives a little shake of his head. "Never mind, it's ungrateful and it doesn't matter."

I feel his thumb on my hand slowly caressing my palm. Our fingers are interlaced now, our hands placed between our chests.

I reach over with my free hand and run my index finger across the prickly stubble on his jaw. He makes the tiniest noise, in the back of his throat, and I know it's want, because I want too. I want him so badly right now that I physically ache. I shouldn't. I'm the one who begged him to leave me be, told him we could only be friends. But that was before. Before he opened up to me, before I saw that he could be more than the box I'd put him in. I realize that he was never that guy—the inconsiderate rich guy. He was Niko, and I think Niko might actually be pretty fantastic.

"It does matter," I whisper. "Just because your family is rich doesn't mean you're never allowed to want things—other things, different things. I'd like to hear about it. It matters to me."

He raises our joined hands to his lips and presses a sweet, soft kiss to my knuckles. My breath comes in short, fast puffs as I watch his eyes.

"You're making it awfully hard for me to be only a friend," he says, his voice wine-soaked sex.

My chest heaves, and everything south of my belly button tingles in anticipation. "Maybe I'm rethinking that particular rule," I answer.

His eyes turn hot, his lips part. "Oh yeah? I was afraid—the other night—that my text would upset you. I don't ever want you to feel like you did that night in the club. Like I'm pressuring you to do something you don't want to. I'm your boss, and if we're being smart, we shouldn't do this." There is a tension that's nearly palpable now, and he's strung tight as a wire, I can almost see the strain of the effort he's exerting to hold himself back.

I pause and think for a moment. I know I shouldn't do it. I shouldn't get involved with my boss. I shouldn't get involved with someone I have nothing in common with. I should stick to my work, my friends and my ordinary life. But there is this anything-but-ordinary man in front of me, and he wants me, and I want him. So badly I can taste it. It tastes like wine and sunshine, olives and starlight. It tastes like Niko, and Niko tastes like the adventure of a lifetime.

"Maybe being smart is overrated," I answer. Then I close my eyes and wait.

CHAPTER SIXTEEN

Niko

ForeignXChange Group

Trish: One word Tess—Attention. Which is Beware *in French.*

Tess's eyes flutter shut and I don't move, watching her long lashes resting on her cheeks. God, she's beautiful. Like an angel in some rococo painting, all soft curves and peaches and cream coloring. I probably shouldn't let her give us the green light. No matter who allows it or doesn't, I have no business kissing my student intern. It makes me seem like some sleazy politician. But I can't turn away from her. I can't imagine *not* kissing her now. It's embedded in my very soul. So I lean forward the last two inches between our faces and press my lips to hers.

She lets out a tiny sigh and I groan in utter desperation. I nip at her bottom lip and feel her smile under my kisses. I touch the tip of my tongue to the seam of her mouth and she opens to me. It sends me over the edge. Raising up on one elbow and angling my head, I kiss her properly. And damn does she kiss me back in all the best ways. Our lips crush against each other and her sweet little tongue dances with mine until I'm lightheaded.

I move one arm to the other side of her so I have her caged in and my chest is resting against hers. And God, her soft, lush breasts feel incredible. My balls ache and I'm panting now, as she wiggles beneath me.

"Am I too heavy," I gasp as I lift my mouth from hers a fraction.

"No," she answers, arching into me and nipping at my lips before she giggles.

"What are you laughing at," I tease as I lick up the side of her neck and take her earlobe between my teeth.

"Oh my God," she moans, rolling her head back so her neck is curved like some sort of exotic bird's.

"You like that?" I hiss, my dick straining against my dress pants.

"There aren't words."

I move back to her mouth and kiss her deeply while I test my luck and run my fingers across one of her breasts. The nipple is already hard and begging for attention, so I palm it and slowly rub in circles. She nearly comes off the blanket, crying out, "Oh!" as she writhes. Fuck, she's hot.

"Do you want me to make you come, princess?" I breathe into her ear.

Her eyes blink open and I look down at her. She's dark promise and sweet reward, and I'm more turned on than I have ever been in my life.

I slowly move my hand down her body, our eyes locked the entire time. When I reach the waistband of her shorts, I unbutton and unzip them. All the while she stares at me, never once breaking eye contact.

Slipping my fingers into the top of her lacy panties I feel the soft silky hair there. Then I move lower, until I reach her clit, and rub it with my finger, dipping into the slick wetness that's soaking her.

"Niko," she gasps.

"You're so wet, so perfect." I slide my finger up and down her slit, then inside of her. She presses against my hand and I know that it's not going to take much. I can't help but thrust my dick against her hip as I stroke her.

I use the heel of my hand to push against her clit, and with my finger I find that tiny rough patch inside of her, rubbing it at the same time. She sobs and her whole body goes rigid, everything freezing in place for long, silent seconds. Then she cries out, "Yes!" and I feel her muscles contracting all around my hand, in wave after wave of hot, sweet, release. I capture her cries with my mouth, thrusting my tongue inside of her too.

As she comes down, I soften the kisses, until I'm giving her gentle pecks on the lips, and I take my hand away. My balls hurt, and my dick is on fire, but I'm the happiest I've ever been, because I made Tess happy, and suddenly, I feel like I've found a new purpose in life.

"You're beautiful," I tell her. She gazes at me with a tiny smile, and it lights up my world. I'm so overcome all I can do is bury my head in the crook between her neck and shoulder and breathe her in. I haven't even come myself and what I feel is so much more intense than what I've ever felt with another woman.

Her slender fingers drift through my hair as she looks at me and licks her lips. "We probably shouldn't be doing this," she tells me. "But for the first time in my life, I don't care." I chuckle and lean down to give her another kiss, but she surprises me and flips me onto my back, her long hair hanging in a curtain around our faces as she leans over me.

"So that's how it's going to be, huh princess?"

"You have no idea," she answers, before unbuttoning my dress shirt, planting delicate kisses along my chest and abs as she goes.

"Fuck, that feels good," I gasp. She brushes my shirt aside and gazes at me, her eyes hot with desire as I sit up with her straddling me and shrug out of the shirt. "Now it's your turn."

Her smile is wicked as she slowly lifts her own blouse and lets it slide over her head before dropping it to the deck, leaving her in only a skimpy, red satin bra, the cups cut so low I can see the dusky pink skin around her nipples.

She's a vision that works its way from my chest where my heart thumps time and a half, down to my dick that throbs at the same pace—I take in her shiny, gold hair waving around her shoulders, contrasting with the deep red of the bra. Her breasts are the perfect size, full and round, and her waist is tiny, hardly any bigger than my two hands.

I skim my fingers over her shoulders, awed at how fortunate I am to experience this with her. The light scent of the saltwater drifts in the air, and I hear the waves washing ashore on the adjacent beach. My lips meet with hers, and in my soul I get the same feeling— the feeling I have when I'm on the water, when I'm sailing and the wind is rushing, the water spraying, I'm part of something powerful, something bigger than me. I've never felt this anywhere but on the water, but I feel it *here*, with her, and I know that I will never sell this boat. Ever.

"Are you sure about this?" I ask.

She tilts her head to give my lips more access to her long, smooth neck. I chuckle as I lick her like an ice cream cone.

"Mmm," she moans. "I'm sure that I want you to do more of that."

"Oh princess, I'll do as much of that as you want."

I feel her hand slip between us, and she grasps my dick through my pants. I jerk, my balls tightening and sending tingles all the way up my spine.

"Jesus," I moan as I cup her face in my hand and lean my forehead against hers. "If we're going to keep this up I think we need to go below deck. How about it?"

Before she can answer me a shriek followed by giggling drifts toward us. Then we hear heels thudding along the dock. A second later Christos's voice snaps me out of the lust-induced haze Tess has me in.

"Here," I grab her top and hand it to her, reaching down and trying to zip up her shorts. She's still straddling me, and she's moving too much as she fumbles with her top. I lift her off of me and stand, dragging her up at the same time. She's gotten her arms through the sleeves, but still has the front of the shorts unbuttoned when Christos appears at the front of the boat, flanked by two girls decked out in club clothes—mini skirts, lots of cleavage, sky high heels.

I grab Tess and shove her behind me, giving her a chance to button up. My shirt's still open, and my pants are tented a mile high, but hopefully in the low light Christos and company won't notice.

The girls are hanging off of Christos's arms, and he's whispering to one of them while she giggles.

"C," I say, using his old soccer nickname. "What are you doing here, man?"

Christos's head jerks up, and he pauses, craning to look to one side of me before a smirk spreads across his face.

"Hey, bro. These lovely ladies and I were going to hang out, have a few drinks." He sways on his feet, obviously drunk. "But I see you have company. Who's your little friend?"

I can feel Tess huddled against my back, her head nestled between my shoulder blades. She's not offering to reveal herself, and for some reason I don't want Christos to know it's Tess. This, being here with her, feels like something fragile, something special and unique that's all mine. And I realize in that moment that she might be the only thing in the whole wide world that *is* all mine. Not my father's, not my family's, mine. And right now, I want to protect what's mine.

"So you party on my boat without me often?" I ask, deflecting so I don't have to answer his question.

Christos stiffens, seeming a lot less drunk than he did two minutes ago.

"No, man, we were wandering by is all. It's no big thing, right? We didn't mean to interrupt your private event. But, hey, more is merrier. Why doesn't your guest join us? I bet you've got some champagne below, we can chill, help keep the girls warm." His two companions giggle more and wrap themselves around him like octopi.

"Yeah, maybe some other time?" I try to put the warning into my voice so he'll understand that I'm not in the mood for this right now. "I think I'd like to keep my party private."

He puts his hands up like I've got a gun on him. "Got it. No problem, we'll head out, maybe go to the house. Come on ladies, you can see Niko's place. He's got the biggest television on the island."

I give him a thumbs up and the three of them disappear down the dock out of sight.

I hear Tess mumbling behind me and finally turn around to look at her.

"Oh hell," she squeaks. "Did he really not see me?"

I put my arms around her, rubbing her back lightly. "No. He couldn't tell who you were. I'm..." I don't know what to say about this, or even what I feel. "I'm sorry he interrupted. I don't know what he was doing here."

"It's okay," she says, stepping away from me and leaving me chilled on the outside and the inside. "We sort of got carried away, right? I mean, it was probably for the best..." Her voice fades as she looks up at me from under her lashes.

I take her hand and walk us back to the bench along the edge of the deck. When we sit I pull her onto my lap and hold her close.

"I don't think so. I think that may have been the best thirty minutes of my life."

She chuckles, her breath warm against my neck where her head is tucked. "Says the horny guy."

"Hey, I'll freely admit I've got blue balls right now, but that's not why I said it." I gently push her away so that I can look her in the eyes. "I like you, princess. I always have, and the more time I spend with you the more I like you. That was the best thirty minutes of my life because I got to know you better, I got to make you smile…" I take a deep breath, trying to control my raging hormones. "And watching you come will fuel my fantasies for months."

If the light were brighter, I'm sure I'd see her blush.

"Oh wow," she moans as she buries her head in my shoulder again.

I laugh. "So. Can I ask you something?"

She nods.

"When you said you didn't mind breaking the rules with me—did that mean tonight? Or would you be willing to do some rule breaking in the future too?"

A small smile curves her lips as she watches me. "I have to give you props," she says, her voice low and rough. She runs a finger down the skin on my chest that still peeks out from my unbuttoned shirt. "You're pretty persuasive in the rule breaking department."

"Oh yeah?"

"Mmhm. I could probably be persuaded to break them again."

Things inside my chest are dancing around. "You're right though about the work stuff. We'll need to keep the rule breaking to ourselves. My dad's not going to get angry, but he asked me not to, and I don't want you to feel uncomfortable. I know I'm asking you to place a lot of trust in me. I want to be worthy of it. I think you're worth the risk."

She thinks about this for a moment. "Okay," she says finally, and relief washes through me like warm spring rain. "Not at work."

"Not at work," I repeat. I pull her closer to me then and lean down to kiss her. "But we're not at work now."

"No," she whispers as her eyes flutter closed. "We're definitely not."

CHAPTER SEVENTEEN

Tess

ForeignXChange Group

Tess: Paisley, do you have any of Degas' work at the Hermitage? His series of ballerinas are the most romantic paintings I've ever seen.

I stumble into my apartment at seven a.m., and am greeted by a very pissed and very tired Cass.

"Where the hell have you been?" she snaps as I shut the front door.

"Oh! You're home." I go to the couch and flop down, exhausted, but deliciously so. "I figured you'd be at Anton's."

"Well, I'm not. He had to visit his grandmother in Athens, so he's gone for a few days. But I had no idea where you were. You didn't answer your phone, and I've been up half the night worried about you."

I leap off the sofa and run to hug her. "Oh, Cass! I'm sorry. My phone died and I'm so used to you being gone I didn't even think that there might be someone waiting for me at home."

She gives in to my hug even though I know she'd like to stay pissed. "Okay, it's all right. But next time you're out all night give me a heads up."

"I promise." I go back to the sofa, putting my feet up, closing my eyes and getting ready for a nice early morning nap.

"So. Where were you?"

I open one eyelid to see Cass standing over me with a wicked gleam in her eyes. Oh shit.

"Ummm…"

"Out with it," she demands.

I sigh and sit up. "Fine. I was with Niko."

"Oh. My. God!" She jumps up and down and puts her hands over her mouth. "Seriously? Niko? Your boss, Niko? Billionaire Niko? Hot as hell Niko?"

I nod slowly, a grin taking over my face. "Yeah. And he was amazing."

"You slept with him?!" Cass nearly breaks glasses with her high-pitched shriek.

I put my hands over my ears and shake my head vehemently. "No! No, I didn't sleep with him."

She collapses on the sofa next to me. "Well why the hell not?" she asks, a pout on her puffy lips.

I can't help but laugh at her antics. "I'm not really a first date kind of girl."

"Was this?"

"Was this what?"

"A first date? Because if it was? Congratulations, superstar. Niko's not exactly known for dating if you get my drift."

"Ugh. I don't want to hear about it."

"But answer the question—was last night a date?"

"No. I mean, yes. Well…no."

"Tess?"

"Okay. It didn't start off as a date. We ran into each other after work and had a friendly walk together, ended up on his boat and one thing led to another."

"Another what?"

I laugh again. "I don't kiss and tell."

"Come on," she whines as she tucks her feet up under her butt and gives me her best puppy dog eyes. "You spent the night with one of C-TV's most eligible bachelors of 2014, you've got to give me something here."

I sigh, thinking about Niko's hands on me, his lips, his skin. "We uh, you know, had quite a bit of fun. I guess you could say his boat is really great."

"Ooh, ooh! Did you *rock* it?" She laughs hysterically at her own joke. Yeah she's one of those people.

"We might even have rocked it more if his cousin hadn't shown up all of the sudden. Those two are weird with each other, I don't understand that whole thing."

"Christos? You know he's Niko's deftheri, right?"

"Yeah, he explained that to me. And I like Christos, but something between the two of them seems off sometimes. Like maybe Christos isn't as happy being the consigliere as everyone thinks he is. I mean, who would want to spend their whole life voluntarily coming in second to someone else?"

"It's not quite like that." Her face scrunches as she struggles to explain. "In that family it's a huge honor, they've been doing it for generations. In any Greek family everyone accepts their place. You're used to it from birth, you know? But in the Stephanos family if you're going to live with an assigned role, being the deftheri is the second best one you can have."

I think about it for a moment. I can understand it, even though it's very different from the family I grew up in. "It's not so much the idea that I doubt," I tell her carefully. "There's something else. I can't really put my finger on it."

"But you obviously put your finger on some other things last night," she answers, busting up into laughter again.

I roll my eyes before shutting them. "I've got class in a couple of hours, but it's nap time now," I mutter as I drift off to the sounds of Cass listing off all the things I might have put my fingers on last night.

**

The regret takes about twenty-four hours to set in. An email from Nate doesn't help matters any.

To: TessR@chiu.edu
From: NR280@fbi.gov

Hey Mess. What's going on in Greece? Mom said your classes are hard. You can do it though, you're the best student in the family. Mom and Dad would have crapped their pants if I'd ever gotten grades as good as yours.

I met this guy the other day who's with Anderson and Blakely here in DC. They're one of the biggest accounting firms in the country, and he said they use a lot of forensic accountants. I asked if you could send him your resume, see if maybe they'll have any internships next summer, and he told me definitely. They've hired a couple of people out of Chicago University's program in the last few years. So, get that to me ASAP. We want to send it to him while he still remembers.

You suck,

Nate

I stare at the screen, the guilt galloping around my insides like a herd of wild horses. I'm risking it—my future. I'm risking it for a hot guy in Greece. It's a cliché, a stupid, adolescent thing to do. But it feels like so much more than that. When I look in his eyes, touch his skin, when he smiles at me or calls me princess, it feels like it's real, like it's so much more than a fling on an extended vacation.

The deal is, I don't do many things for myself. Sure, I'm majoring in accounting because I chose it, but I chose it in part because it's something that would make my family proud, would earn enough so my parents don't have to help me after school, would give me the resources to help them if they ever needed it. I picked Chicago University not because it was my first choice—that was actually a school in Colorado where I could learn to ski—but because it gave me the best scholarship. I didn't want my parents to have to borrow money to send me to school.

I do lots of things like that—I follow the rules, and I work hard to keep my family happy—and I don't mind, because my parents and my brother are my favorite people in the world. They've earned my best, so I make sure to always give it to them. But every once in a while I wish that I could do something for me. Something that I didn't have to choose to please them, or to prove anything, or to be practical. Coming to Greece was sort of supposed to be that thing, but when I decided to take an extra full load of classes, and do a half-time internship I didn't really think that I'd taken the joy right out of the whole thing.

Now there's Niko, and he's like a big, two hundred-pound muscle-bound package of joy. He makes me feel things no one ever has. He makes everything seem more—more colorful, more intense, more fun. Like I've been living a life in pastels, and he's suddenly come and thrown a rainbow of vibrant colors over everything. I'm not sure that pastels will ever be okay again. I'm not sure that I can give this up. I'm not sure that I care about the rules anymore.

I'm about to close up the computer when my phone chimes, and speak of the devil, there's Niko's name.

Niko: Hey beautiful. I'm thinking about you.

Me: Sweet talker.

Niko: I hope you aren't regretting our rule breaking.

Me: Are you?

Niko: Absolutely not. As long as you're happy, I'm happy. I wish I could see you though. I'm stuck at a family thing right now—my nephew's birthday.

Then he sends me a picture of him with a tiny baby lying on his chest. My ovaries explode.

Niko: This is my second cousin, Andrea. She's three weeks old. I'm her godfather.

Me: You're so much sexier with a baby on your chest.

Niko: I'll take her with me everywhere from now on.

Me: Until she gets a dirty diaper anyway.

Niko: Well, that killed the mood. Lol.

I send him a picture of me lying in my bed, surrounded by my schoolbooks.

Niko: And that brought it right back. Can I see a closer shot of those shorts you're wearing? Damn.

Me: rolling eyes. Perv.

Niko: Seriously? I'm a guy. Your shorts are tiny. And you're not wearing a bra.

Me: How the hell can you tell that from a photo?

Niko: It's a special talent.

Me: I may need to see more of your special talents.

Niko: I am so happy you said that. Oh shit. One of my sisters is screaming for me. I've got to go play soccer with her kids. See you tomorrow?

Me: Yes. Have fun with your family.

Niko: Not as much fun as I'd have with you, princess. I'll be dreaming about you.

Me: Good night.

Niko: Sweet dreams.

**

School has gotten rolling and the coursework is piling up. Between the part-time internship and the full-time class load I haven't had a second to breathe in days. Niko and I see each other in passing at the office, and we've texted more, so things aren't uncomfortable, but I don't know if we'll actually ever have a repeat of the night on his boat. If I had time to be sad about that I would be, but I've slept about five hours a night since then, and I'm lucky if I get to eat twice a day much less three.

I'm walking out of my last class of the day when I hear my name being called from across the lawn. I turn around and see Niko jogging toward me, a big basket of some sort in one of his hands.

"Hey," he says when he reaches me, his hair mussed from the breeze, and his jaw darkened with a day's growth of stubble. Stupid, sexy stubble.

He lifts his glasses and rests them on top of his head. "I'm glad I found you. Cass told me what time you got out, but I don't know the campus that well and all the main office would tell me was that the business majors are on this side of the complex."

"What are you doing here? Is there some emergency at the office you need me to help with?"

He puts his free arm around my shoulders and starts walking, herding me along with him. "No. In fact, you aren't coming into work today."

"What? Why not?" Shit. I've screwed something up and he has to fire me. No, no, no.

He pulls me against his side and squeezes my shoulder. "Stop imagining horrible things." How did he know? "You've been working too hard and I can tell you don't eat or sleep enough so I brought you food and we're going to have a picnic and spend the afternoon together."

I stop and pull away to stare at him. "Don't you have work to do?"

"Nothing that can't wait until tomorrow."

"Don't I have work to do?"

"Again, nothing that can't wait."

He gives me a soft smile. "I haven't seen you except in the hallway at the office for days. You promised you'd break the rules with me some more. I've come to collect. Play hooky and let's enjoy the sun for a few hours." Then he leans down and gives me a soft, sweet kiss on the lips, and I'm done for. Plain and simple. He didn't buy me an expensive gift, or take me to some ritzy party. He showed up at my school, with food, and asked to spend the day with me. It's absolutely average, and stunningly special at the same time.

I kiss him back, lingering a moment longer than he did, wrapping my hand around the back of his neck where I feel the short, silky hair that curls up along his hairline. "I would love nothing more than to spend the day with you," I say.

"Is that only because I have food?" he murmurs, gazing into my eyes.

"Of course," I answer, without missing a beat.

We both laugh and he puts his arm back around me as he leads me to the parking lot.

**

I'm in my bra and underwear on the deck of Niko's boat. He motored us out to open water, set anchor, and we've been basking in the sunshine eating pita, cheese, olives, grapes, and chocolate for the last two hours. Since the trip was a surprise, I didn't have my swimsuit, but the bra and panties are working fine. Better than fine if Niko's undivided attention is any indication.

He strokes a hand up my side as he hovers over me, resting on his elbows to one side while I lie on my back. Sunglasses are covering my eyes and I'm trying to get a tan.

"You're blocking my sun," I mumble sleepily.

"Mmm," he answers, licking around my belly button and setting off little sparks in my core. "You're going to get burned. I'm saving you from looking like a lobster."

I wiggle under his mouth and hands. "I'm going to be the pastiest, palest person in Greece."

His lips reach my chest and he pauses. I lift my sunglasses up an inch and squint at him as he stares at my breasts in the peach satin bra.

"Niko?"

"What? Sorry, I didn't catch that." He licks his lips and my heart races.

"You're not going to let me get a tan, are you?"

He pushes up, his bare chest flexing as he climbs over me, trapping my hips between his knees. My heart keeps up its ridiculously speedy rhythm and the air in my lungs rushes out with a sigh as I look at him above me.

He's a Greek man, so his chest isn't bare the way most of the popular male models are these days. But he has just the right amount of hair, warm and silky, swirling around his pecs, then racing in a line down the center of his torso to the swim trunks he wears low on his hips. I can't stop myself from reaching out to run a finger along the trail that makes its way from his breastbone to his belly button.

His voice is rough when he grabs my finger and holds onto it. "I don't see pasty. I see peaches." He softly strokes my breasts over the smooth satin. My nipples pebble and I moan quietly. "And cream," he continues, caressing my stomach with the flat of his palm. He plants his hands on either side of my head, looking down at me with a heated stare. "Come below deck with me so I can get that pretty skin out of the sun."

I swallow, knowing there's a very comfortable bed below. Am I ready for this? It's not the actual act itself I'm worried about, it's what it will mean to me afterwards. I'm in grave danger of falling for this Greek tycoon, and if his kisses are any indication, he's going to rock my boat and then some. Will I be able to keep my heart safe if I sleep with Niko? I doubt it. Can I live with that? I'm not sure.

"Tess," he whispers as he leans down and plants tiny kisses along my jawline. "No pressure, we'll only do what you want, but I need to hold you. I want to feel you. I've been dreaming about you in my arms for days."

Whatever willpower I have dissolves like salt in water. "Yes," I gasp. "Yes."

Below deck we fall onto the double bed that's built into the cabin. It takes up most of the space, with a small galley left for a kitchenette.

Niko's kisses start off slow and soft. We lie on our sides, facing each other, simply breathing in the same air, gazing into each other's eyes. He gently cups the back of my head to draw me closer and dusts his lips across mine. Soon his tongue slips out and I take it into my mouth, sucking as he moans and crushes his lips against mine. We deepen the kiss, tongues tangling and breaths coming faster, harder.

"You're gorgeous," he pants as he slips his thumb under the fabric of my bra and teases my nipple. I spear my fingers into his thick hair and pull him closer, craving the feel of his skin on mine, wanting nothing more than to absorb him, make him part of me.

Soon he pushes my bra aside and his mouth meets my nipple. He sucks, swirling his tongue around the areola at the same time. I gasp from the electricity that shoots through me. Like a live wire that runs from my breast through my heart and then down to my core. While he plumps the breast he's sucking with one hand, his other presses against the seam between my legs, nudging my thighs apart.

Through the tiny round window that illuminates the cabin, I can see slivers of us. His hand, my flesh, his hair, my pink nails. The sounds of our breaths mingle with the soft murmur of the sea outside and the occasional call of a gull overhead. The combination of sights, sounds, and caresses is erotic, deep and sensual in a way it's never been with another man.

"Niko," I cry out as he slips his hand inside my panties. I grab his wrist and stop him.

"I'm sorry," he gasps. "Tell me what to do. I'll stop if you want."

I don't want him to stop, but I'm overloaded, and I'm scared. Scared to lose my heart.

"No...I don't know." I shake my head from side to side and try to collect my thoughts.

He cups my cheek and looks at me with such care and warmth my poor overworked heart nearly bursts.

"It's okay, we don't have to do anything. I can just hold you."

"I want you," I answer. "So badly."

He grins. "The feeling is mutual."

I play with the hair on his chest while we whisper, following the little curls and patterns.

"I'm scared. I'm falling for you and if we do this—"

"If we do what?" he asks, a wicked smile on his face.

"If we have sex," I clarify.

"Mmhm," he rumbles from deep in his chest.

"I'm afraid you're going to break my heart."

His smile drops like a rock in a deep pool. He blinks at me once, twice, then his eyes drift closed and he lays his head alongside mine, his mouth next to my ear.

When he speaks his breath is hot and I shiver from head to toe.

"Oh, beautiful Tess. You have no idea what you do to me, do you?"

I shake my head and feel his tongue dart out to touch my earlobe.

"Trust me, the only one who's at risk of a broken heart here is me," he says. "I'm falling for you so hard it feels like I'm drowning some days." He lifts his head and watches my face, gently moving a lock of hair out of my eyes. "And I'm ready to give up and let the water take me."

CHAPTER EIGHTEEN

Niko

ForeignXChange Group

Darla: Romantic paintings? Like the ones of that Greek party god where everyone's naked and boning, and he's feeding them wine?

Tess smiles, a knowing, cunning grin, then she pulls my mouth to hers and kisses me like there's no tomorrow. I've gone and done it. Given her all the power. Told her that she can wreck me if she chooses. And it's okay. Because I've waited my whole life for this—for her. For something that *I* chose. Something that I will have to *work* for, every day. Something that is all *mine*.

Before long we've stripped off our remaining clothes and she's straddling my lap on the edge of the bed, her hot, wet center wedged against my raging hard on while I alternate between devouring her juicy mouth and sucking on her ripe tits.

She thrusts her hips against me and I nearly burst right then. "I want to be inside of you," I growl.

"Please," she answers. I reach into the side table and grab a condom. She takes it from my hand and does a very sexy tear of the foil with her teeth, eyes on me the entire time.

"Can I tell you something?" I ask as she reaches between us to roll it on.

"Please," she repeats.

"You're the best fucking intern I've ever had."

Her laughter is like a burst of sunshine in a rainstorm; fast, bright, and utterly beguiling.

I take advantage of the break in action and roll her under me. Her thighs part and I settle myself between them, my hunger for her roaring to the surface with demands that I pump, hard and fast.

I draw back and she shifts to align us, then I push in. It's the hottest, sweetest thing I've ever felt.

"Jesus," I grunt when she wiggles underneath me.

"You have to move," she gasps. "I need you to move."

Never one to ignore a woman's request, I start to move, in and out, savoring every thrust, every retreat, every tiny breath that escapes her as she develops a rhythm with me.

My balls tighten even more, and I know I won't be able to hold on long. "Tell me you're close, baby."

"Yes," she answers. I reach between us and press my thumb to her clit, and she flies apart, convulsing around me like a velvet vise. I follow right behind, my orgasm like a damn semi-truck that's lost its brakes. It's hard and fast, and long, and when it's over I can hardly move, much less think.

I roll off of her and lie there, my heart pounding like I've flat out sprinted for days.

She tucks herself into my side and I trail a fingertip along her back, unable to speak for a few moments.

"Wow," she whispers.

"Yeah," I reply.

When I think my legs won't give out on me I get up and dispose of the condom, stopping to look at myself in the mirror of the head. My hair is a jumbled mess, and I need a shave already, but my eyes are bright, and I can't help the smile that won't subside. I scowl at my reflection for a moment, trying to contain the adrenaline that's pumping through my veins. But I can't. And I know why. As frightening as it is, and as much as I never thought it would happen to me, I know what this is. I've found the thing that my life was missing, the something deeper, something better, something more that I've been craving. I've found it and now I can't lie, I won't lie. I have to admit it, to myself, if not to anyone else yet.

I've fallen in love with Tess Richardson.

**

My boat becomes a sanctuary for Tess and I. We spend every possible moment there, and on the days we can't meet up, I feel this grating sense of dissatisfaction, as if something is fundamentally incomplete with my life.

I've just had one of those days today. It started with meetings with our legal department about the quarterly audits. For some reason the American IRS is giving us crap about our records for shipping in and out of Los Angeles. By lunch I'd moved on to a personnel dispute between my second cousin Raoul and his ex-girlfriend, Nina. My father insists on keeping all family personnel issues handled by family. So this one won't be going to H.R. But it is proof positive that you shouldn't fuck people you work with, and a reminder about my tenuous situation with Tess that makes me more than uncomfortable.

Tess came in after lunch as she normally does, but I was stuck in my office with our head of security over some bullshit attack that happened to one of our ships off the coast of Somalia. Fucking pirates. It's really not my job to deal with security issues, but our operations officer was out of the office, and I was the only chief executive his secretary could track down. The head of security didn't look all that happy to see me, but he gave me the basics anyway. The ship had been moving more of these medical supplies that we seem to be shuffling all over the world, so it was discouraging to hear that we'd lost something that might have been needed by good people.

I spent a large portion of the meeting watching Tess at her desk outside my office window. I never used to keep the interior blinds open, but I find myself doing it more and more just so I can have a look at her. I'm like a kid standing outside a candy shop with his nose pressed up against the glass. I can see it all, nearly smell it, almost taste it, but never really reach it. I'm finding it more and more difficult to concentrate at work with her only a few feet away, yet miles in terms of practicalities. Maybe this is the real reason they say not to get involved with someone you work with. It's a little like being Tantalus in the bowels of Hades.

By the time I'd ushered every needy employee out of my office, it was well after the end of the day and Tess was long gone. I texted her to see if she could meet me, but she was in the middle of a study session with some classmates. Now I've come home, and I'm exhausted, cranky, and lonely, not necessarily in that order.

"What's up, man?" Christos asks as he comes into the living room rubbing a towel across his head. He's obviously just come from the shower, and he's bare-chested, his hair damp and his feet shoeless beneath a pair of designer jeans.

I'm slouched on the sofa with my tie off, my shirt untucked and a bottle of beer in my hand. "Long-ass day," I reply.

"I've got the perfect solution," he says. "Go change into some club wear and we'll hit ladies night. There are going to be hundreds of hot women trolling for drink specials."

I glance at him from under my eyebrows. Christos and I haven't been right for weeks now, we gloss over it, but things haven't been the same between us, and I know he feels it too. I've spent my whole life with him, knew him better than I knew myself sometimes, but now, after twenty-four years, I'm painfully aware that these days I don't know him as well as I thought I did.

In spite of that, I want to fix things with him. He's my brother, and I love him. The problem is, I'm not sure how to do it when I'm keeping things from him—

namely my relationship with Tess—and while we haven't discussed it, I feel pretty sure that Tess wouldn't like the idea of me picking up other women at bars while I'm sleeping with her. I damn sure know I'd have to put my fist down some guy's throat if I found him with Tess. All of this means I'm going to have to say 'no' to Christos's invitation and that's going to piss him off.

I take a long swallow of my beer. "Yeah, not tonight, but thanks. I'm too wiped out."

Christos scowls at me and crosses his arms. "Do you know how long it's been since you and I went clubbing? Or did anything together for that matter?"

I keep my eyes on the label of the beer bottle in my hand. I can't look at him, because he has a point.

"I know, man, I really do…"

"Come on. I won't even chase any skirts. It'll be you and me. We'll have some drinks, argue over the World Cup lineup." He sits down next to me and leans forward, elbows on his knees. He looks at me sideways, his expression earnest, the usual crowd-pleasing Christos banished for a brief moment. "I want to spend some time with my brother," he says quietly. "Not to be girly, but I kind of miss your ugly ass."

I don't look at him, but I can feel his eyes on me, and I smirk, knowing it'll piss him off. "Aww, that's so special, baby," I croon. He slugs me in the arm. Hard. "Fuck. All right all ready. I'll go out with you, but no chicks. And no discos, I can't stand a whole night of that fucking bass. Let's shoot pool or something."

He grins. "Pool it is. I'll whoop your ass and you can buy all my drinks."

"You wish," I shoot back.

"You're getting old," he says as he walks back to his bedroom to finish getting dressed. As if eight months makes me substantially older than him. "You don't stand a chance."

CHAPTER NINETEEN

Tess

ForeignXChange Group

Tess: Screw it. I'm getting the fish and chips.

It's nearly ten o'clock when I get done with my economics study group. I'm exhausted and starving, and all I want to do is dissolve into my bed with Netflix and a bowl of cereal. Unfortunately, when I walk into my apartment Cass is bouncing off the walls and Anton is not far behind.

"You're here! You're here!" she cries, leaping across the room and grabbing me in a hug.

"You're drunk! You're drunk!" I reply, mocking her.

"Not even close. Just a wee bit tipsy," she gushes, arm around my neck as Anton chuckles from the sidelines.

"What have you been feeding her?" I ask him, one eyebrow raised.

"We've been at the café down the street…"

Oh. The one with the ouzo that'll knock you on your ass faster than Rhonda Rousey. "Did he let you get the ouzo sampler?" I ask Cass, rolling my eyes. She loves the ouzo sampler, but she shouldn't be allowed to have it. It makes her crazy.

"Maaaybe," she sings.

"God, Anton, how could you? It's Thursday night. She'll never make it to class in the morning."

He shrugs. "She's funny after the ouzo sampler. And frisky too," he adds, wiggling his eyebrows.

Cass giggles before leaving me to throw her arms around Anton's neck. "Oh yes I am, baby." She kisses him all over his neck and jaw, and his grip on her hips tightens, making her moan.

I put my hands over my ears and scrunch my eyes shut. "Stop it, stop it, stop it. Ugh."

Anton laughs again and I open one eye to see if the coast is clear. He's peeled Cass off of his chest and has her contained, her back to his front, his arms locked around her waist.

"The best thing we can do is get her sobered up," he answers.

"Yes." She nods her head up and down seriously. "Must get sobered up."

"And how do we do that?" I ask, finally going to the living room and dropping my book bag on the floor.

"We go to a bar," she exclaims.

**

Somehow the convoluted logic of taking a drunk woman to a bar to sober her up has landed me at this pub near the campus. Anton swears the greasy food will help keep Cass from the pain she was sure to feel tomorrow morning, and Cass refused to go unless I came along. The place is packed, apparently there's a special on both shots and fish and chips, so every college student on this side of the island has decided to stop in.

"We're never going to find a table in all of this," I tell Anton as he leads us through the mess of tables, stools and people.

"I've got a friend who works here," he answers, looking back over his shoulder. "I texted him, so he's saved a table for us."

Sure enough, we get to the far side of the room, and there's a table with a big reserved sign sitting on it. It's in a great spot, right next to the pool tables, and not too far from the bathrooms, but out of the main traffic pattern.

"Well done," I tell Anton as we all sit down.

"Thanks," he says. "Only problem is we're going to need to go to the bar to get our order put in."

"I'll do it," I say. "You stay here with her."

"I'm not deaf you know," Cass pipes up. "I might be ouzoed, but I can still hear when you talk about me like I'm not here."

"Ouzoed?" I ask, trying not to laugh.

"Whatever," she slurs before leaning her head on Anton's shoulder.

Anton takes out his wallet. "Grab us two fish and chips plates and a couple of waters," he says, handing me forty Euros. "I'll take a draft beer too. The guy you want to order from is Stavros." He points toward the bar. "See him with the black t-shirt?"

I stand from my chair so I can see over the heads of the people at the table next to us. Sure enough, behind the bar is a tall guy with dark blonde hair in a black t-shirt.

"Yep, got it. I'll be back in a few minutes," I tell them. Cass mumbles something and Anton and I grin at each other. She really is a funny drunk.

After I nudge and squeeze my way up to the bar, I spend a few minutes trying to get Stavros's attention. But I'm short and the bar is tall, so finally I jump up and down when he's turned my direction, waving my arm in the air and shouting his name.

He leans over the bar, watching me with a grin. "Well, hello little elf. What can I do for you?" he asks.

"I'm a friend of Anton's," I tell him. "He said to order with you?"

His smile grows. "You're Tess."

"Yes!"

He looks at one of the guys on a barstool next to me and says something to him in Greek. The guy doesn't look very happy and snaps back at him, but Stavros waves a dishtowel at him and the guy slides off the stool, gesturing for me to take it. I give him a smile which he doesn't return before he stomps off. Once I'm settled on the stool, I'm finally tall enough to look Stavros in the eyes. They're very nice brown eyes, and they go well with his blonde hair. He's got a Jensen Ackles kind of thing going on.

"Make yourself at home, Tess." He rests his elbows on the bartop in front of me, looking a little like a friendly wolf. Then he pours a shot of something amber and slides it toward me. "For Anton's pretty friend. On the house."

I smile politely at him. He's cute, but he's not Niko. "Oh, I probably shouldn't. I've got school and work tomorrow."

"That's top shelf tequila," he tells me nudging it closer. "It's the smoothest stuff on the planet and I promise it won't give you a hangover."

I look at the pretty liquor and then around the room at all the other college students drinking, dancing, making out. It's hard sometimes, always doing what you should, instead of what you want. And right now I want to have a drink, relax, maybe flirt—just a tiny bit—with the cute bartender.

I reach out and grab the shot glass, wink at Stavros, and toss the tequila back, wincing at the burn as it travels down my throat before it lands in my stomach warming me from head to toe.

"Atta girl," Stavros chuckles. His hand reaches toward me ostensibly to take the shot glass back, but he manages to hook a couple of fingers around mine. "Now, what can I get for you?"

"You can start by getting your hands off of her," a voice says behind me. I twist in my seat to discover Niko glaring at my hand in Stavros's.

I yank my hand back. "Hi. What are you doing here?"

He glances down at me, his face softening a touch. "I could ask you the same thing."

"Mr. Stephanos," Stavros says, his hands well on his side of the bar now. Cass wasn't joking, everyone on the island does know Niko. "What can I get for you?"

Apparently Stavros has forgotten that I was here first.

Niko's jaw tenses again. "You can get the lady whatever she needs and put it on my bill. Then you can get me a Septem ACE," he says imperiously.

Stavros has a weak smile as I tell him my order, then he slinks off like a dog who's been scolded.

The space around me has magically emptied, and Niko slides in to the bar, standing next to my stool and rotating it so I'm facing him.

"I see the prince of the island is back," I mutter, one eyebrow raised.

"You're kidding me, right?" he snaps.

I scowl at him. "You scared the crap out of Stavros and he was only doing his job."

"And his job included touching you?"

I open my mouth, then shut it again, not sure how to respond to that.

He leans forward into my space, taking a good portion of the air with him apparently since I gasp like a fish out of water. His fingers capture my chin, holding my gaze to his. "That wasn't the rich boy talking, that was the jealous one," he rasps, watching my every movement like a hawk with its prey.

"We haven't talked about this stuff. If we're seeing other people and that whole…thing," I whisper, my eyes glued to him as well, my heart racing like that poor little rabbit's about to be eaten for raptor dinner. Because, well, mostly what we've done is have sex.

Great sex. Lots of great sex. I sigh, momentarily distracted.

"Let me make it simple for you," he says. "I don't want anyone else, and I don't want you with anyone else either."

Nothing like bluntness to clarify a situation.

My throat is dry and I swallow before I can answer him.

"Okay," I finally squeak out.

He spears his fingers into my hair, pulling me closer. His lips hover over mine. "We may not be able to go public at the office, but I have no interest in sharing you with anyone."

"I like that," I breathe out before he kisses me, his lips firm, his touch insistent.

Someone clears their throat near us, and Niko breaks the kiss, staying mere inches from my face, his hand still cupping the back of my head possessively.

"Sorry, Mr. Stephanos," Stavros says. "But the lady's order is up and I wouldn't want her food to get cold."

Niko gives him a quick nod. "Have that delivered to my table in the back," he instructs. He glances at me, and I furrow my brows at him. "Please," he tacks on, a smirk working its way across his face.

Niko follows me back to the table Anton and Cass are at. I introduce him—Cass pats him on the cheek and tells him he's a good dog—then he invites us all to sit with him and Christos at their table.

I never have a chance to ask him how we're going to act in front of Christos. He's Niko's best friend, but he also works with us. How is this supposed to work? I have a headache before we even sit down.

Once we're settled and everyone's been introduced, Niko throws an arm around my shoulders and relaxes, a big smile on his face. Christos takes one look at us and a scowl lodges itself in between his eyes. I wiggle uncomfortably, trying to dislodge his grip, but he only tightens it. I see Anton raise an eyebrow at me across the table where he's supervising Cass as she shovels in the fish and chips.

"We weren't supposed to let people at the office know," I grit out as I lean my head toward Niko's ear. "In case you've forgotten Christos is one of those people."

"He won't say anything." Niko grins.

"He obviously doesn't approve."

He turns to me, so freaking pleased with himself. "Hey, we got this. I promise. He's pissed because it was supposed to be the two of us having a guys' night. He doesn't care that you and I are seeing each other."

"Actually, *he* might," Christos says from the end of the table.

Niko levels a look at him and I feel my cheeks start to burn.

Christos shrugs. "Sorry, either you're not that quiet or I'm not that deaf."

Niko doesn't shift in his seat even a touch, continuing to rub his thumb up and down the patch of skin where my top meets my shoulder. But I feel his body tense, his muscles tightening, and looking at his face in profile I see his jaw muscle twitch.

"You need to step down," Niko says quietly.

"Why?" Christos asks, leaning forward with his elbows on the table, his expression determined.

"Because you want a yes man instead of a true deftheri?"

Now Niko removes his arm and rotates toward Christos. "Don't be a fucking dick," he warns.

Christos snorts. "You know what I think of your choices right now, but you don't want to hear it. I can't do what I'm supposed to if you won't let me."

Christos's voice has gotten progressively louder, and Anton is shooting daggers at me from across the table now. Even Cass has stopped eating and her still somewhat foggy eyes are darting between Christos and Niko.

"You need to go walk it off, brother," Niko says, his jaw grinding more. "I'm not going to do this with you right here."

Christos stands up abruptly, tipping his chair over. It clatters to the floor loudly. He gives the table a shove at the same time. Cass squeaks and Anton yelps, "Shit!" as their plates slide into their laps.

Before Niko can stop him Christos has stomped off, shoving a few guys out of his path along the way.

What. The hell. Was that?

Niko wraps his hands around the edge of the table and carefully pulls it back into place.

"I'm sorry," he says, running a hand through his hair in frustration. He glances at me then back to Anton and Cass. "My cousin's normally a great guy. Maybe he's had more to drink than I realized." He darts a look at me. I'm so shocked I just stare at him. "Please let me pay to get your clothes cleaned."

"It's not necessary," Anton says, but I can tell he's pissed, and his lip is curled in disdain as he looks at Niko and slowly picks pieces of fish from his lap and replaces them on the plates. He keeps one hand on Cass the whole time as if he's worried something else will come flying at them and hurt her.

Cass stares forelornly at the mess on her plate. "Damn," she says. "I wasn't done yet."

Anton pats her on the back. "It's okay baby, I'll get you some ice cream on the way home." He looks at me. "Given the greasy clothes and all, I think it's time for us to take off..." He shifts his gaze between Niko and me, unsure of how to proceed.

"Can I get you a taxi?" Niko asks.

"No, we drove," Anton answers.

"Then I'll get Tess home," Niko jumps in.

Anton still looks irritated. "You okay with that, Tess?" he asks.

I almost say 'no'. Niko has been lording it over everyone since I ran into him. The least he could have done was ask me if I wanted him to take me home. But then he leans over and whispers in my ear. "Pretty please?"

Ugh. I'm such a sucker for him. He smiles shyly at me, and I can tell he knows he overstepped.

"Fine," I grit out of the side of my mouth. "Yes," I tell Anton. "I can get a ride home with Niko."

He and Cass get their stuff together and give me hugs and kisses goodbye. As he leans into me, Anton says, "If you need anything at all, call me right away. I"ll get you no matter what."

I smile and thank him. "I'll be fine," I promise. He still doesn't look convinced.

When Anton and Niko shake hands, there's some sort of guy thing that goes on between them. I can see it in the way they grip each other's hands too tightly and look hard at one another. At this point I'm so pissed at boys I just want to go home and sleep for the next two days. Idiots. Every one of them.

After they leave, Niko pulls me up from my chair and envelops me in his big arms. "Sorry about all of that," he murmurs in my ear as he sways a bit to the music playing in the bar.

"What the hell was that?" I ask, my body stiff as he tries to get me to dance with him.

He stops and looks down at me, cupping my cheek in his hand tenderly. "I honestly don't know, but I think it had a whole lot less to do with you and me than it did with me and Christos. We haven't been getting along. We either avoid each other or argue. I'm not sure what the problem is."

"You shouldn't have sprung this—us—on him like that. I think his feelings were hurt as much as anything."

He sighs and pulls me closer. I give up the rigor mortis routine and melt into him. "You're probably right. And I did make him promise no chicks tonight. It was supposed to be him and me. A guys' night so we could catch up, get back in our groove."

"Then you fucked up, buddy."

"Yeah. I did. When I saw that bartender all over you I couldn't help myself. I got all caveman and then I just wanted to show everyone in the damn place that you belong to me. I don't get to at work all day and it's driving me crazy. I really am sorry, princess."

"You should be," I tell him without any real heat because he's now nibbling on my earlobe and I can't think.

He chuckles.

"But this stuff with Christos? It scares me, Niko. We have enough working against us. If Christos is fighting us too, I'm not sure we can survive that."

"Hey." He leans his forehead against mine. "I will handle my cousin. He'll get past this. I'll tell him I'm sorry for not making more of an effort to hang out and I'll make it clear to him he has to accept this—us. It's not his decision. You're not his choice, you're mine. He'll have to learn to live with it, and I have no doubt that if he gets a chance to really know you he'll like you a lot."

"Okay," I answer. It occurs to me though that I'm learning something about breaking the rules. The more you break the harder things get. You upset the status quo and it complicates everything. The dominoes start to tumble and there may not be a way to stop them. I set Niko and I on this path, and from what I can see it's only going to get harder.

"Come on princess," he cajoles. "Don't go weak on me now. You and I are breaking the rules together, remember? And we're going to come out the other side victorious. I'm your prince, right?"

"You actually sound like some ancient Greek god," I tell him. "They were always tempting poor mortal women into horrible decisions."

He plants a soft kiss on my lips. "You can take the man out of Greece…"

"Can you take this woman out of the bar?" I grin at him, his kisses and even his ridiculous posturing getting all of my girly parts warm and tingly.

"Let's go." He grabs my hand and leads me out.

We walk into the cool night air, and right away I can smell the ocean that laps at the edge of the island a few blocks away.

"Should we go to the boat?" Niko asks. "I'd take you to my house, but I don't feel like dealing with Christos yet."

I nod in agreement and we set off along the cobbled walkway down the hill to the waterfront. We haven't gone even ten yards when we hear a strange sound from one of the many small alleyways that line the larger street.

I lean closer to Niko. "What was that?" I whisper, peering into the dark of the narrow passage.

"Sounds like maybe somebody passed out," he answers. "Probably just a drunk."

The groan comes again, followed by coughing and a gruff, "Fuck."

"He sounds like he might be hurt. Should we check?" I ask.

"*We* aren't going to check anything," Niko says, stepping in front of me. "*I* will though if that's what you want."

"Be careful," I admonish. He looks at me over his shoulder like I'm an idiot, then pulls his phone out of his back pocket and turns on the flashlight, stepping into the alley.

"Shit," he says. "Christos?"

CHAPTER TWENTY

Niko

ForeignXChange Group

Kellie: There was an explosion at the feis you guys. An actual bomb. I've spent my whole life waiting to dance at worlds, and now I'll never have the chance again.

Christos is a bloody mess, his face bruised and scratched, his nose dripping blood, and his knuckles shredded where he holds his hands in front of his eyes to shield himself from my flashlight.

"I got jumped," he croaks out before I rush forward to kneel in front of him. I hear Tess's shoes clacking on the pavement as she runs into the alley behind me.

"Oh my God," she says as she reaches us and takes a look at my best friend.

"Who the fuck did this?" I demand.

"I don't know, man," Christos gasps, clutching his ribs. "They came out of nowhere."

"We've got to get him to the hospital," Tess says.

I hoist Christos to his feet, wrapping his arm around my neck to support him. I hand Tess my phone to call an ambulance, but Christos stops us.

"No. I'm okay. I don't want to go to the hospital."

"Now's not the time to be noble, man. You're seriously fucked up, you need to be checked out. There could be things broken, internal bleeding."

Tess's eyes are big but she's tough, and she nods in agreement. "He's right, Christos. You have to see a doctor."

"Take me to your dad's," Christos tells me. "He'll get the family doc to take a look."

I look at Tess, and she shrugs, as unsure of this as I am. I sigh. "Okay, but if he says you need to go to the hospital, you're going."

Christos grunts in agreement and I ask if he thinks he can make it to the car where we left it around the corner. He nods and we slowly make our way to his Maserati GranCabrio. After loading him into the back seat I reach for the passenger door to help Tess in.

"I'll get a cab," she says, putting a hand on my arm.

"No, it's late and whoever did this to him could still be around."

"It'll take you too much time to drop me off, you need to get him to your dad's."

I open up the door. "Yeah, and you're coming along. I'll drop you off later. Is that okay?"

She purses her lips. "Isn't this sort of a private family thing? Christos doesn't even like me. I'm sure he doesn't want me there for all of this."

"But you're not here for him. You're here for me. I want you with me." I tuck a strand of hair behind her ear and I realize that they aren't simply words. I do want her with me, no matter what might happen over the next few hours. I want Tess to be with me for it. I want her in my parents' home, talking to my family, listening to our business. It's scary, but I do want it.

"All right," she answers. "Whatever you need."

"Thank you." I give her a short kiss on her sweet lips and we get in the car and head out of the city.

**

My parents' villa is about five miles out of town, on a precipice that juts out from the cliffs above the ocean. The original building has been there for hundreds of years in one form or another, and it's where my father was raised and my grandparents still live. Dad built a second house when he took over the family business, and I grew up there. It's a typical Greek design, lots of white stucco and blue accents, window shutters, wooden doors, terra cotta stairs outside and inside going from one level to the next.

I phone ahead to warn them we're coming and my dad calls the doctor right away. He doesn't question Christos's decision to forego the hospital and I'm somewhat surprised by that.

We pull up in the long winding driveway that ends with a parking circle made of cobblestones.

The place is lit up like Athens, and I'm sure it's in anticipation of our arrival. The moment I turn off the ignition my parents, Cara, and my dad's security guys rush out to the car. They're in such a hurry to get to Christos that no one seems to notice Tess, who stands next to the passenger door silently watching the commotion.

"My darling boy," my mother cries when she gets a look at Christos. "Who would do this to your beautiful face?" She cups his cheeks. "Cara, run and make sure the blue bedroom is ready for him."

"I'm okay, *Theia*," Christos chokes out.

My dad has his security guys take Christos from me, and they move him toward the house as Pop turns to me, his eyes lighting on Tess briefly before he addresses me.

"Your *Theia* and *Theios* are on their way," he says, referring to my aunt and uncle, Christos's parents.

"And the doctor?"

"Should be here in a few minutes," Pop answers. He looks at Tess again, reminding me that I've been rude.

"Pop. This is Tess. She was with me when we found Christos." I turn to Tess. "This is my father, Ari Stephanos."

My brave girl steps forward and extends her hand, a warm smile on her face. "It's such a pleasure to meet you, Mr. Stephanos."

"American," my father says. "And very lovely," he adds, giving her one of his charming smiles as he takes her hand and holds it between his two palms. "Thank you for being there to help my nephew and son."

"Of course," she answers. "I only wish I could have helped more."

"Come. Come inside. Both of you. We will have some wine while we wait for the doctor and then maybe you two can help cheer up Christos."

I spend the next forty-five minutes splitting my time between the lounge with my father, and the bedroom Christos is laid up in where my mom is softly talking to him and cleaning up his wounds. I take Tess to the lounge where she opens up an eBook on her phone and assures me she'll be fine. Christos looks better already getting all the dried blood washed off, but he's going to have some serious bruises.

We listen to my dad tell stories about his stint in the Greek navy as well as the first few times he tried to do business in the US. It wasn't always smooth sailing, in either job.

When the doctor finally arrives, my father asks me to keep Tess company while he goes in to hear what the doc has to say to Christos.

"He's charming," Tess says after he leaves the room. "I see where you get your tendencies from."

I chuckle. It's true, my dad is one hell of a salesman. It's tough to resist him no matter what he's suggesting.

"He liked you," I tell her. "I can tell."

"Does he know I work for him?"

I shake my head. "No, but I'm sure he'll have questions about you now that he's met you."

She nods, brows pinched in thought. "Do you think this was such a good idea? I understand that Christos is supposed to go along with whatever you want. I don't think it's very fair, but I get that's how you guys do things. But your dad? What if he says I have to leave the company?"

I stand and move from my chair to the sofa where she's seated. "I probably should have discussed it with you first." I've made one error after another tonight. I'm trying to be the good guy Tess wants, but it's hard. I'm not used to having to check with anyone else when I make a decision, and all I want is to keep Tess with me—everywhere all the time, damn the consequences.

She picks up my hand and shifts to face me. I want to lean forward and suck her beautiful lips into mine, taste their sweet berry flavor.

"Now that he does know, we need to decide how we're going to handle it."

I scratch the back of my neck, wondering how to balance all of these people and their various demands— Tess asking me to be honorable, Christos asking me to be easy, my dad asking me to be the heir, whatever the hell that might entail. I've been ignoring what's going to happen if Tess and I kept seeing each other, but she's right. We can't act like this is a normal situation. There are landmines everywhere.

I lay my head on the back of the sofa, face turned toward her. "Do you have any suggestions?" I ask, secretly crossing my fingers she's got an answer to all of this.

"It's *your* family," she scolds.

"I know." I take a deep breath and put my bravado back into place. "I will explain it to my dad. I'll tell him that this isn't me screwing someone at the office. You're important and we're seeing each other, and we're being discreet. He's going to have to get used to this. I promised you this would be okay and I won't let anyone, not even my family, hurt you, Tess. I swear it."

I stroke her hand with my thumb, then lean forward and place a small kiss on her lips. "I know I'm a handful, but I'll never stop trying to redeem myself and be the guy you want me to be," I tell her.

"Mr. Stephanos?" The doctor leans his head into the room.

I stand and go to greet him. "Yes. How is he?"

"Your cousin is going to be fine. He received a bad beating, but nothing's broken, and there are no signs of concussion or internal organ damage."

"Thank God," Tess says as she joins me.

"He's not going to be up and around for a few days. In twenty-four hours he can start taking regular anti-inflammatory painkillers. In the meantime I've prescribed something stronger. Your mother's been given the instructions for his dosage. I'll be back to check on him tomorrow afternoon."

"Thank you, doctor." I shake his hand again and my dad's security guy, who's been hovering nearby, shows him out of the house.

I turn to Tess. "I should go see him."

"Yes. Absolutely. I'll be right here whenever you're done."

I can't help but lean down and kiss her again. "Thank you," I say, my voice low and gritty as my throat is thick with relief for Christos.

"You're welcome."

**

When I get to the hallway outside of Christos's room I hear him talking to my father. I'm about to turn the knob on the door when I hear my dad say, "You're sure it was Arabic they were speaking, and they mentioned the shipments to Syria?"

"Yeah," Christos answers. "I recognized the tattoo one guy had on his hand. It was the same one Malik had. And the part about Syria was crystal clear, no matter what language they were speaking."

I grip the knob tighter, but then my dad's voice rumbles out again, "Not a word about this. To anyone. You did the right thing telling Niko you didn't see them. I'll say I've filed a police report. We'll tell the office the same story."

"Okay," Christos says. "What are we going to do about it? Do you think they'll try something else?"

"I'll have the security detail deal with that. You don't need to worry. But I want you handling those accounts personally from now on. I want you there every step of the way. You need to be at the docks checking the arrangements for each of those shipments. Up the security, double-check the contents. We can't let a shipment go wrong again. Understood?"

"Yeah. I got it."

"Good boy," my dad says.

I pull my hand back from the doorknob. I'm shaking and my throat is dry, parched, the tang of fear coating my mouth. I turn and dive into the bathroom next door when I hear my father's footsteps coming closer. He leaves Christos's room as I slide down the door on the inside of the bathroom, putting my head in my hands and wondering what in God's name I've just stumbled into.

**

I spend ten minutes trying to clear my head. When I finally stand from the floor I have to follow my gut and it tells me that this is serious shit and I can't unhear what I have. But until I figure it all out I'm not going to say a word. I'm disgusted, sick, and torn to pieces, but I won't let them know it, because they'll only lie more. They've obviously been lying to me for a very long time.

I step into Christos's room and he's already fast asleep, undoubtedly pulled under by the lure of prescription painkillers. I watch him for a moment, thinking about a lifetime of brotherhood, of trust, and shared objectives. When did it stop being about the two of us together? When did he become indispensible while I became nothing more than a figurehead, a mascot to prop up for public consumption? The pretty, fun, stupid one. They might as well have given me a crown and a sash for all the importance I actually have. I swallow the bile down, and leave the room. The room where the true heir sleeps.

**

When I enter the lounge my dad is entertaining Tess again. I've lost my taste for his charm, however.

"It's late," I say as I walk in and reach for Tess's hand. "I need to get you home."

She looks a little surprised by my abruptness but she takes my hand and stands anyway.

I turn to the man who's professed that I'm the most important thing in his life for twenty-four years. The man who's been lying to me for God knows how long, and probably would have continued to forever if I hadn't overheard what I did tonight.

"Please tell Mom goodbye for me."

"Of course," he says, his eyes tired. "We'll see you this weekend?"

"I'll let you know," I hedge. "Let's go," I say to Tess. She thanks my father for the visit, and I take her to the Maserati. Once we're in and headed down the long driveway back to the main road she asks, "Was everything with Christos okay?"

"He's going to be fine."

"Are you sure? You seem tense."

I take a deep breath, lifting my shoulders then dropping them. "Just work stuff. I have to figure out how to get Christos's projects covered while he's gone." And lies beget lies. Because they lied to me, now I'm forced to lie to Tess, and I hate it. It's like a secret dose of poison has been released into my bloodstream where it will slowly make its way through my body, killing cells and turning flesh black as it goes.

I look at her beautiful face, and realize that she might be the only real and true thing in my world right now.

"Come home with me?" I ask, nearly breathless with the weight in my chest.

"Are you sure? It's so late. Maybe you'd rather get a good night's sleep?"

I grasp her delicate hand in mine, feeling the tiny bones that link together so perfectly to create the work of art that is her long fingers, soft palms, and smooth skin. "All I want is to hold you all night long," I whisper.

She leans over and kisses me on the cheek. "That sounds wonderful," she answers.

CHAPTER TWENTY-ONE

Tess

ForeignXChange Group

Tess: I'm so sorry Kellie. So terribly sorry.

I don't see much of Niko's house when we get there.
The lights are off and he leads me quietly through the
winding hallways and cavernous rooms to his suite.
Inside is a king sized bed, made up with snowy white
linens and a dark duvet. One side of the room is glass,
French doors opening to a patio that surrounds the
swimming pool. In the moonlight I can see the water
lapping at the infinity edge before the whole landscape
spills over to the beach below.

He's silent as we walk to the bed, and once there he
gently kisses me, pushing my top up and off before

unbuttoning my jeans and dropping to his knees to peel them down my legs. He removes my heels, then pulls my feet from the tangle of denim gathered around them. As he stands back up he runs his hands along my skin from ankle to shoulder.

"You're so gorgeous," he whispers, coasting his lips along my neck.

I sigh, my hands finding the buttons on the front of his shirt and popping them open one by one. I trail my fingertips across the taut skin of his torso and he shivers, dropping his head to my shoulder as I caress him. I sense that he needs this—my touch, my silence—and I give it to him, because I'm starting to realize that there isn't anything I wouldn't give to him. And that scares me more than I could have ever imagined.

When we're undressed, Niko lays me on the soft bed and worships me. His hands are butterfly soft, his lips like angel wings brushing against me tantalizingly, moving from one place to the next with no order or strategy.

When I'm finally writhing under him, my breath harsh and needy, he takes a condom from the nightstand and rolls it on. As he looks down at me, his weight on his elbows, his lower body cradled between my thighs, he whispers, "I think I'm falling in love with you, Tess Richardson," then he slides into me and my world ceases to be anything beyond this room and this man.

We make love slow and soft and sweet. He strokes in and out of me, his breathing stuttered, his brow shiny with sweat. I arch into him, the slide of our skin sultry and decadent. "God," I whisper. "So close."

He lowers his head and kisses my lips—full, wet, deep—and I come, waves of ecstasy rolling through me over and over. He pushes deeper than he's ever gone, as if he can enter my very soul, and then gasps, pulsing inside of me until he collapses, his heat and sweat like the most beautiful blanket I've ever laid under.

His head is buried in the crook between my neck and shoulder, and he's trembling. I don't know what's happened, but I do know that the prince of Georgios is suffering. Between the time we entered his father's house and the time we left, something went very wrong, and I'm not sure what to do to make it better for him. So I do the only thing I can. I stroke his hair, his back, his shoulders. I wrap myself around him until his shaking stops and I feel him relax. When he finally rolls off, he gazes at me deeply before he says, "I meant it." I swallow and nod, knowing full well what he's referring to.

I open my mouth to respond, but he places a finger over my lips. "It's too soon, I know that. Don't say anything. I just needed you to know."

I kiss him gently, my hand cupping his scruffy cheek. He turns me to face away from him and then wraps his arm around me. He buries his face in my hair and finally falls asleep.

**

When I get to a computer the next day there is an email waiting for me from my brother.

To: TessR@chiu.edu
From: NR280@fbi.gov

Mess: First off, Mom says you need to send her your social security number so she can fill out the annual health insurance forms. And Dad says to tell you that Snickers ate one of his shoelaces and puked all over your room. Then he went on his annual rant about how this was why you shouldn't have gotten a cat when you were only going to go to college and leave it for him to take care of.

I'm glad you're having a good time. You need to send more pictures. There's this agent that I'm angling to ask out, and she loves to travel, so your pictures give me an excuse to go to her office and show her. Give your big brother a break and help him with his game (no remarks about the quality of my game either you runt).

You haven't talked much about the internship. Are you able to understand everything they need you to do? By the way, you haven't seen anything unusual in the way they do stuff, have you? You know I can't talk about the details of an ongoing investigation, but I can tell you that the IRS is doing an audit on their US operations. Have you heard about that? I want you to be very careful that you don't do anything you have any doubts about, even if your boss says you have to. I can help you out with your bills if something doesn't seem right about the job.

Got to go, Mess. Try not to miss me too much. I know it's hard when your older brother is such a hunk of sizzling manhood. No one you meet ever lives up to what you've been raised with. But don't worry, I'll be nice to your boyfriends even if they are pussies. They

*can't help it. Just like you can't help it being an
undergrown runt.*

    You suck,

    Nate

I can't help but laugh when I read his nonsense. Nate is built like my dad, linebacker big. Over six feet and especially since Quantico he's one big block of muscle. But he has a baby face, and a personality that's midway between class clown and computer nerd. No woman is ever going to mistake Nate for a hot alpha guy even if he sort of looks like one.

His continuing warnings about Stephanos Shipping and their business practices is starting to grate on my nerves. Nate doesn't know that I'm seeing Niko, mostly because I think he'd flip the hell out. He's protective under the best of circumstances, and me a few thousand miles away dating the son of a Greek billionaire who is also my boss would not go over well.

But I can't tell him that he shouldn't talk to me about these things with Stephanos. If I found out that Stephanos might be doing illegal things, how am I supposed to explain that to Niko? I can't up and quit if something is fishy. I could never be the one to tell Niko that his family's company is unethical or God forbid, criminal. So, I do what I've been doing for weeks when Nate harps about Stephanos Shipping's business—I write back, tell him it's all fine and try to forget that he ever told me any of it. I hate it. It goes against everything I've been raised to live by. If there's the merest whiff of something unethical going on, I should quit. My reputation will be of paramount importance in my career, and I can't be associated with a business that might be cutting corners.

But here's a side of the sleeping-with-your-boss coin that I never once predicted. What happens if *you* don't want to work for *him* anymore? Luckily I'm not at that point, and I can only hope it doesn't happen. First, because I wouldn't feel right about taking money from Nate, and secondly, because I'm afraid it might break Niko's heart.

I still don't know what happened last night at his dad's but he's not okay, no matter what he says. When we said goodbye this morning he was distant, quiet. Not at all himself. I can only hope that it was some sort of posttraumatic shock from finding Christos in that alley. I guess the next few days will tell.

When I walk into the office Annais and Juliet are whispering at the front desk. They look up when I walk in then motion me over.

"Hey. What's going on?" I ask.

"You won't believe what happened last night," Juliet whisper shouts.

"Shhh," Annais admonishes. "Christos was mugged and beaten outside a bar downtown."

I swallow. I hadn't thought about this, and Niko and I forgot to talk about it. I'm going to have to lie more. I can't admit that I was there with Niko when it all happened. It's like it never ends.

"That's horrible," I say. "Is he going to be okay?"

Juliet nods. "Yes, Mr. Stephanos—Ari, not Niko—made an announcement this morning on the employee loop. He said that Christos is recovering for the next few days and he'll be back in the office next week, but he wanted everyone to be very careful when they're out downtown after dark. They haven't caught the guys that did it."

"Do they have any leads?" I ask, genuinely curious.

"No. Christos didn't even see who it was. He doesn't remember anything. Mr. Stephanos says if anyone was in the area last night they should contact his head of security."

"I don't think they're going to find anything," Annais says, shaking her head. "It's high tourist season, whoever did it has probably gone back to Athens or whatever tour of the EU they're on. I guarantee no one on the island did this."

Juliet shivers dramatically. "I've never been afraid after dark here, but now? I guess I'll have to find men to escort me places."

I'm sure that's no hardship for her. She doesn't strike me as the type who's got a problem manipulating men into doing things for her.

Then she glances at Niko's office door.

"That ship sailed," Annais says with a snort. "Maybe you can get Niall in Media to walk you around town at night." She laughs and Juliet sticks her tongue out at her. Everyone who's worked at Stephanos for more than a week knows that Niall has a ridiculous crush on Juliet. He's up on our floor at least three times a day. Usually he asks Juliet some stupid question and then stands there and gazes at her star struck while she answers.

"I'd better get to work," I say, hoping that I don't have to hear Juliet refer to a renewed pursuit of Niko. "Will there be a card or something for Christos that I can sign?"

"We're putting together a basket of things to keep him entertained. I'll bring you the card to sign, and you don't need to contribute, you're a student, that wouldn't be fair," Annais says, smiling at me.

"Okay, thank you. I hope he gets better fast."

"Me too," Annais says, her eyes so serious. "These kinds of things don't happen in Georgios, and especially not to one of the Stephanos family. It's gotten everyone pretty shaken up."

An hour or so later I'm sitting at my desk reviewing records for shipments in and out of Athens during the previous month when Niko comes walking through on his way to his office.

"Tess?" he asks, pausing at my desk.

I look up at him trying not to show how happy I am to see him. "Yes?"

"May I see you in my office for a few minutes? I have a project I think you can help me with."

I nod and grab a pen and paper before I follow him into his office. He doesn't speak or look at me, but goes straight to the interior windows and shuts the blinds, before walking to the door and locking it with a decisive click.

When he spins to look at me his face is wrecked, my beautiful prince is suffering and I can't help but bleed inside for him.

"What's wrong?" I ask as I move toward him.

He takes a decisive step forward and wraps his arms around my waist, lowering his head to mine and devouring my mouth with single-minded determination. I'm stunned at first, but I melt into his touch out of habit, loving the way he tastes like the rich espresso he must have been drinking at lunch. He smells like the ocean and I wonder if he ate at Andropov's near the water.

As we settle into the kiss and his hands begin to roam, my head clears a little and I remember where we are—his office, in the middle of the workday.

I break the kiss and try to lean back so I can see his face. "Hey, I thought we agreed not to do this at the office."

He kisses my neck, avoiding my gaze. "I think. We need. To rethink. That," he mutters in between kisses, nips and licks.

My traitorous body leans into his, craving his every kiss and caress. "That sounds dangerous," I gasp.

"Mmhm," he growls as he palms my ass with one hand and pulls out my hair clip with the other. "Dangerous can be exciting. We're getting really good at breaking rules, let's break some more."

My gut clenches. Rules. Those things that insure your life stays in control, help you reach your goals, and keep you safe. Until I met Niko rules were so simple. So easy to follow and so comforting to understand. But now, since I started breaking them, what once was black and white becomes more muddled with each passing day. I know Niko feels strongly about me, and I feel just as strongly about him. I'm falling for him and it's scary, but also the most exhilarating thing I've ever known. I don't want that to end. I don't want to deny Niko anything. I don't want to deny myself anything, so I turn those little blinking warning lights right off. Lock them up tight and throw away the key as I throw myself into Niko's clutches.

"You're a terrible influence," I whisper to him as I take his earlobe in my teeth.

He presses his hard on against me, the steel of his length firm and huge even through his dress pants and my skirt.

"Is it working?" he asks.

"Totally," I admit.

He growls and walks me back to the desk behind us. When I'm pressed up against it he kisses me hard before spinning me around and pressing me flat to bend over the warm wood.

"I've dreamed about this," he says in my ear as he folds over my back and reaches under me to grasp my breast.

"You're not the only one," I sigh.

CHAPTER TWENTY-TWO

Niko

ForeignXChange Group

Foster: How's this for a small world you guys? I just ran into my best friend from high school, here—in England. Too bad we hate each other now, right?

I spent my lunch listening to my father grill me about Tess. Christos was kind enough to answer all of my parents' questions about who Tess was and how I met her, and my dad is not thrilled.

He seems to think that with a father who's a district attorney and a brother with the FBI, Tess is more likely to want to pursue some sort of employment action against us if I do something to piss her off. With what I suspect about our business operations, I doubt he's really concerned about something as minor as a personnel action.

The hypocrisy of my father busting my chops about dating a staff member is beyond the pale, and I could hardly keep from telling him so over lunch. Everything he said made bile swirl in my gut. I ended the conversation by telling him to stay out of my private life. He reminded me of the promise I'd made to him. I told him Tess was different, and it wasn't up for discussion. He has no right to criticize my choices, not after what I think he's done.

Now I'm standing behind Tess, her gorgeous ass in front of me as I bend her over my desk. Lucky me, she's wearing a thong. Fuck, she's amazing. I squeeze the two firm globes in my hands and moan. I push her against the edge of the desk harder and her hips flex in response. Unzipping my fly I release my swollen dick, aching to plunge into her and drown myself in the only thing I know will make the pain stop for a while.

I lean over and whisper in her ear, "Don't make a sound," before I tug her thong to the side and drive in, causing us both to gasp at how fucking good it feels.

As I move in and out I'm nearly paralyzed by pleasure. She's the warmest wettest thing I've ever been in, and it's about to short circuit whatever brain cells I have left.

She reaches an arm behind her and grabs my ass, clawing at my flesh, her breaths coming fast and hard. I drive into her a few more times, and I can tell she's close, so I fold over her back, pulling on her hair to lift her head off the desk. Her neck is arched and it's all I can do not to lean in and bite the shit out of it. "I want you to fucking come for me," I murmur in her ear as I push into her hard. Her beautiful lips open on a silent cry, and I feel her spasm around me, that's all it takes to send me there as well, and I pulse into her hot and hard.

When we finally calm down, I rest, softly stroking her hair as I run my nose along the fragrant skin of her neck.

She rises up on her elbows and turns her head so she can capture my lips. "I don't know what the hell's gotten into you," she whispers, "but it's freaking hot."

I chuckle, giving her one last peck on the lips before I pull out. I stand there looking down at my dick. My very bare, very much unsheathed dick. Fuck, what have I done?

Tess adjusts her thong before pulling her skirt down. As she turns to face me her nose crinkles and she shifts around, wiggling her hips a little. "Um," she says, looking at me strangely. I'm still frozen, my hand down my pants where I was tucking my dick away. We stand there looking at each other for a moment.

"I'm so sorry," I say as I finish zipping up. "I forgot, the uh."

"I thought things felt *damper* than usual," she answers, squirming some more.

"God, baby, I am so sorry." I bend a little to look her in the eyes. "I'm distracted and I've been thinking about you all day. Shit." I dig a hand into my hair.

Her sweet hand strokes my cheek. "Hey. Niko?"

I look at her big blue eyes.

"I'm on the pill. It's okay. We're good. We're exclusive—" She looks worried for a moment and I leap to reassure her.

"You heard me at the bar, right? Please don't worry about that. I've never been with anyone without a condom and I haven't been with anyone else since the day I first saw you on the docks. I swear. If you're on the pill then we're good."

She smiles and rubs against me a little like a cat. "So good," she says, an evil look of glee crossing her face.

I grin back at her, the crisis gone like so much dust in the wind, if only the rest of my life would sort itself as well. I put my hands on her hips and smooth her skirt out some more. "Yeah? You had a good time then?" "Quit fishing for compliments," she scolds, and I laugh. "You know that was amazing."

"It sure as hell was. I think we need to make it a regular part of our afternoon coffee breaks."

"We have afternoon coffee breaks?" she asks, smirking.

"We do now," I answer, wiggling my eyebrows.

"I'd better get back to work though. I've got a lot of numbers left to crunch with this account."

"Okay. But I'm giving you a ride home, so come get me when you're done for the day."

"And if someone sees us?" she says.

"I'm allowed to give an employee a ride home," I tell her.

She shakes her head, then puts a hand on my cheek, her eyes tender and a tiny bit sad. "I would do anything for you, break any rule. Please don't lead me into something that ruins me."

Before I can formulate a response she's gone, and I'm left in my office, at a job I don't love, with a company that's poised for collapse, a best friend who's betrayed me and a family who's abandoned me. I may very well be speeding toward my own ruin, and I'm just selfish enough to take Tess with me.

**

I've avoided going to see Christos for three days, but I can't again. My mother is upset, and the guilt is killing me. I leave work early, telling Tess I'll check in with her after I've seen him.

When I get to my parents' house the place is quiet, my dad not home from work yet, my sister still off at a café with her friends after school.

"Niko!" my mother cries as she comes out of the back of the house to greet me. She kisses me on both cheeks and begins talking in rapid fire Greek. "You finally came…you're breaking my heart…what is this you were mad at your father about…" She speaks some English, but since most of her life has been spent on this island raising children, organizing events at the church, and taking care of the family, she doesn't have as much opportunity to speak it as my father does.

"Hi Ma," I say, kissing her back. "I came to see Christos."

She shakes her head and ushers me to the kitchen. "I'm about to bring him his tea, you come to the kitchen and then you can take it back to him."

I follow dutifully, bracing myself for more of the inquisition. By virtue of being in boarding school and college abroad for so many years, I've been spared a lot of the Greek mother treatment, but there's no question that mine is a master at it. She can emasculate me, shame me, worship me, and coddle me all in one conversation.

We reach the kitchen with its cerulean blue tile walls and I greet the cook who is already working on preparing an elaborate dinner at the large commercial grade stove in the corner. My mother goes to the marble island in the center of the room and begins setting up a tea tray, including a coffee and extra food for me.

"No coffee for Christos," she admonishes as she gets the briki out and starts measuring coffee and water. Then she pulls out the sugar, putting one level spoonful into the mixture. "He'll try to take yours, but he's still recovering. He needs the healing herbs in the tea."

"Okay, Ma," I tell her, trying to hide my smile.

"Now," she says as she bustles around digging out biscuits and honey. "Why is it that your deftheri has been here on his sickbed for days and yet you've not come to see him once?"

Yeah, I knew this was coming. I had plenty of time to come up with an excuse, but did I? Hell no, because no Greek guy wants to plan out how to lie to his mother. I default to the only thing I can. "I'm sorry. I got busy, and I should have made time to come sooner. Forgive me?"

I give her my most charming smile, the one I've been practicing since childhood. She makes a small sound of disapproval as she flips on the burner in the island cooktop and puts the briki on it to heat. "I may forgive you if you come to church on Sunday and stay for dinner."

At least she's predictable. "Of course, Ma. Anything for you."

She beams at me and pats my cheek some more. "My beautiful boy. You make me so happy," she says. The guilt stabs through me like a dagger to the gut.

She's quiet for a moment, watching the coffee as it heats. I brace myself for whatever's coming next.

"Your father tells me you were angry with him at lunch," she says.

I run a hand across my chin, feeling the five o'clock shadow that's already filling in. "I think Dad needs to stay out of my love life."

"Even when your love life is taking place in the middle of his office?" she asks.

"Look, Mom, I don't want to argue with *you* about this either. When was the last time you saw me date anyone more than twice? You're the one who's always asking why I can't find a nice girl and settle down. Well, Tess is a nice girl and I'm not ready to settle down permanently, but I do want to be with her for now. I can actually see a future with her, you know? That's never happened before."

She puts her hand over her mouth, her eyes soft as she nods her head a couple of times. "You love her," she whispers.

I feel my face flushing. I can only hope Christos is in bed where he belongs so he isn't hearing all of this. I'm about to lose my man card.

"I don't know. I might," I mumble.

I look up at her from under my scowl. She leans over and kisses me on the forehead. "Then that's all anyone needs to know. I will talk to your father and tell him to leave it. You can't help it that the girl works for you."

I break out into laughter. This is the part about being Greek that Tess can't understand, the part I've tried to explain to her. It's not that we don't have rules, it's that they're sort of situational, and if you don't like them, you simply ignore them.

"Thanks, Mom. Maybe you can put in a good word for me with Dad."

She nods and I know that she'll do it. She'll hassle my father until he gives in, and hell, he of all people shouldn't care about messing with a few rules, God knows he isn't playing by them.

Finished with the tea tray she lifts it and hands it to me. "Good. That's settled. Now you go apologize to your cousin and everything in our family will be right again."

I sigh. If only she knew how wrong she is. But I will shield my mom from this for as long as I can. I know it will kill her if she ever finds out.

"Okay. I'll say goodbye before I leave."

"Good boy. And next time you have these problems you come to your mother. You're never too old for me to fix things for you."

Greek mothers.

**

Christos is sitting in an armchair watching some old Die Hard movie when I enter his room.

His face is a bloom of colors—blue, black, yellow, green, and a smattering of purplish-red across one cheekbone and the underside of his chin. His left wrist is wrapped in a bandage, and his hair is combed back off of his face on one side where a line of stitches run from his temple into his hairline.

"Jesus, bro," I say as I enter and set the tray down on the end table next to his chair. "I didn't realize you still looked this banged up."

He glances at me for a split second before returning his eyes to the TV. His face is impassive, no sign that he's heard me.

"How could you?" he asks rhetorically. "You haven't seen me since it happened."

He's pissed. But the thing is, so am I, and I don't feel like groveling to get him to forgive me. Not when I suspect he's violated *my* trust a lot more than the other way around.

"Yeah, sorry about that." I grab the demitasse of coffee off the tray. "It's been pretty crazy at the office."

He huffs out a breath, the disgust practically dripping from him. "And over the weekend? Or do you work seven days a week now?"

I don't bother to sit down because I can tell this visit isn't going to last long.

"I've got a girlfriend, bro. We have *plans* on the weekends." I grin and wink at him, but it's not really friendly, and he knows it. My bitterness is in competition with his disgust, and the room is churning with the combination.

"So she's your *girlfriend* now?" he asks, finally looking at me. "You tell Uncle Ari that? Cause I don't think he's going to be thrilled."

"Don't," I warn him. "Don't go there. I'm trying to be considerate since you're laid up, and I'm sorry that you got jumped, but you need to stay the hell out of my relationship with Tess. And that includes not running to my dad about it. I can't understand what about me and Tess scares you so much anyway."

His eyes narrow and his mouth presses into a thin line. "Scares me? Why the fuck would I be scared of your girlfriend? The only thing that's scaring me right now is how much she's changed you in the short time you've known her. I mean, what the hell have you done with my best friend? The guy I grew up with would never choose a girl over his family."

I can see my hand trembling as I hold the coffee, so I set it down quickly and fold my arms hoping that Christos didn't notice.

I give him my coldest look, putting everything I've got into the showdown. "I haven't chosen anyone over the family, but keep this up and you'll force my hand. I'm not sure why you hate her so much, but you have no justification for it. She's done nothing to you, I've done nothing to you, and we sure as hell haven't done anything that's a danger to the family. You on the other hand…" I stop myself right there, my anger having spilled words I didn't intend.

Christos looks at me sharply. "What? What about me?"

"You're the one who's created this issue between me and Dad," I cover. "You've dragged my dad into this campaign you've got against Tess. It makes no sense, Christos. None of it. Why do you hate her? Why is it so important to you that I don't see her? And don't say it's because of fucking sexual harassment suits, we both know that if anyone were going to get hit with one of those it's just as likely to be you as me. You've dated nearly every woman under the age of thirty in the entire office and half of them in the Athens office to boot." I pause, remembering the first time I took Tess to lunch.

"In fact, you tried to date Tess before I told you to back off. How the hell do you explain that?"

I've got him, and he knows it. I wait to see if he'll come clean, if he'll admit the real reason Tess scares him so much, wait for him to tell me that he and my father have betrayed me and put my entire future in abeyance for reasons I can't even guess at.

I wait.

He shakes his head. "Never mind, man. I'm too tired to do this with you. If you can't see what a problem she is for us then I can't help you."

I watch him for a moment while he returns his attention to the television. He won't tell me. I've given him the perfect opening and he won't do it. A lifetime of friendship, of family, of devotion, and he won't tell me what he and my dad have wrought. But it's there— as clear as glass—a prison they've sentenced all of us to. And while they're focusing all this attention on Tess, who's nothing more than a student intern, God only knows what else lurks out there ready to destroy the things we've all dedicated our entire lives to. Our family, our business, our principles. The resentment inside of me boils over, and I know that I'm about to burn bridges, storm castles, destroy cities.

"I'll have your things moved to the pool house tonight," I say as I walk to the door and turn the knob. "And you can consider your transfer out of Finance a done deal. Just tell H.R. where you want to go." Before I leave I face him again. "If you ever decide to tell me what this is all really about I'm ready to listen. But as long as you insist on hiding behind these baseless accusations and fears, I can't have you as my deftheri. I can't have you as anything."

I shut the door softly after I walk out. I forget to say goodbye to my mother. I forget to do anything but get in my car and drive. I drive until the road reaches the sea, and then I get out, walk to the sand and stand looking out at the waves until the sky turns dark and the sickness in my soul subsides.

CHAPTER TWENTY-THREE

Tess

ForeignXChange Group

Tess: Last time I heard, my best friend from high school was working in a strip club.

I haven't seen Niko in two days and I'm worried. He's returned my texts but he was vague and short. Something about working out of the office and handling some family issues. But I know there's more to it than that. The last time I saw him he was on his way to visit Christos, then radio silence. Knowing how close they are, I have to think something's happened *to* Christos or *with* Christos.

Because of that fear, I'm relieved to walk into work and see Christos sitting at the spare chair in my cubicle.

If he's all right then I have to assume that Niko is as well.

I reach my desk and get my first look at his face. It's bruised, but they're fading, and the cut on his forehead is healing up, the stiches small and neat. Hopefully he won't have much of a scar.

"Hi!" I say, and it comes out artificially chipper. I bite my lip in embarrassment, trying to modulate my tone appropriately. "Um, it's good to see you well enough to come back," I finish as I sit in my desk chair and face him.

He nods, his expression serious. "Thanks. And thanks for helping me that night. Probably wasn't how you envisioned things when you went out to have fun."

I relax a bit into my seat. I'd like nothing more than to have a do over with Christos. I'm not sure why he doesn't like me, but if I'm really going to keep seeing Niko I need to at least try with his cousin.

"I'm happy you're okay," I tell him honestly. "That's all that matters."

He takes a deep breath, thoughtful for a moment. "Can we talk?" he asks.

I laugh. "I think we already are."

He chuckles. "Yeah. But I've got something a little more serious in mind."

"Okay. Of course."

He looks around. The office is pretty empty, most people are still at lunch or just getting back, gossiping and grabbing coffee, before settling in at their desks.

"I think we got off on the wrong foot," he tells me. I nod at him to continue. "I've spent my whole life being trained to protect Niko, advise him, watch over him. I know it probably sounds really weird to you—I tried to explain it to some Americans in college once and they looked at me like I was a creepy stalker." He laughs bitterly.

"I get it," I tell him. "The expectations are somewhat different in the culture I come from, but I get it. I have an older brother and he would do virtually anything to protect me."

Christos's face darkens, but then he gives himself a small shake, almost like he's literally rolling something off his back.

"I think you have the ability to hurt him," he says bluntly. "In ways you don't even realize, and I didn't know how to handle that so I tried to warn him away from you." He scratches the back of his neck, yanking on his tie a bit. "It obviously had the opposite effect."

I blink at him a few times, having no idea what to do with that information. "Why?" I ask, genuinely perplexed. "I mean, how could I hurt Niko? He's the one with all the power here in case you haven't noticed."

He shakes his head sadly. "Then you haven't seen the way he looks at you. It's pretty obvious who has the power, and trust me, it's not my cousin."

I think back to Niko's confession to me on his boat. Christos is talking about an entirely different type of power. "So you're afraid I'll break his heart?" My voice is soft, sad, and I am too.

"Can you promise me you won't?" he asks.

I think about it. Can anyone ever promise they won't inadvertently destroy another person? No matter how much you love someone can you absolutely guarantee you won't hurt them? I don't think so. I don't think it's possible to make that kind of promise. That's why love is risky, why we run from it, and avoid it, and ridicule it, and deny it. It's the riskiest thing you'll ever try with the most essential part of yourself.

"I'm not sure anyone can make a promise like that," I answer, willing him to understand.

"I need you to," he says, his eyes earnest and almost desperate. "No matter what happens, I need you to swear to me that you won't do anything that would break Niko." He pauses. "Please."

"What is this really about, Christos?" I ask. Something here isn't right. He's not telling me everything.

He brushes off my question. "Promise me, and I'll never give him trouble about you again. I'll fix all of this between him and me, but you have to swear to me."

He's so desperate, so focused, and of course I'd never do anything to hurt Niko if I can help it. Never. Maybe if I promise this Christos will be appeased and Niko will come out of hiding?

"Okay." I nod, becoming more convinced as I speak that this is the right choice. "I promise. I won't do anything that would hurt him. His heart is safe with me, Christos. *He's* safe with me."

His relief is visible. He exhales as if he's been holding a breath for long minutes. He stands and puts his hand out to me across my desk. I put mine out to shake, but instead he simply holds my fingertips, looking deeply into my eyes. "Thank you, Tess. I don't deserve it. I don't deserve your pledge, and I don't deserve his friendship, but I'm very grateful for all of it. I'll try my best not to let either of you down."

He drops my hand, then turns and walks away, shoulders hunched and head down. A single tear rolls out of my eye and snakes its way down my cheek. Something terrible has happened to the heir and the spare of Georgios, and it might break *me* to watch.

**

The music is blasting and I know he'll never hear me yelling, but I do anyway, because at least then I can say truthfully that I called out when I barged into his house. Some tiny part of me conjures up all the scenes in movies and TV shows where the girlfriend or the wife walks into the house to surprise her man, only to find him in bed with someone else. But for all that I know Niko used to spend a lot of time at the clubs having one-night stands, he doesn't have a player's personality. He doesn't seek oblivion or validation in women. Still, I'm relieved when I walk through the living room and find him in the home gym, attacking a weight machine with dangerous intent.

"What did that poor machine ever do to you?" I ask as I walk around to where he can see me. He'd never hear me with the 1990s rock blasting from his wireless speakers.

He releases the shoulder press he's been pumping back and forth and squints at me like maybe he can't quite remember who I am. I hope that's not the case. It's only been two days. I'd like to think I'm a little more memorable than that.

He reaches to the armband on his biceps and turns the iPod off. My ears ring in relief. Cloaked in silence after such volume, we stare at each other for a moment. He's shirtless, sweat dripping down between his pecs and around the ridges of his abs. I try not to gawk, but it's a sight that's hard to ignore. A lot of glistening golden skin over perfectly proportioned, steely muscle. Yum.

"Did you?" he asks.

I realize he's been talking to me. I look up to his face and he has one eyebrow raised, a smirk curling up one side of his lips.

"I'm sorry." I clear my throat. "What did you say?"

He stands and stretches, and I feel positive that at this point he's doing it only to torment me. I narrow my eyes at him and he chuckles.

"I asked if you'd been trying to text?"

"Only for two days. And don't you dare say that one response of 'I'm working at home' is adequate."

I'm not sure why I expect an argument, but that's not what I get.

"You're right. I'm sorry."

He moves forward and wraps his big hands around my hips. Giving me the puppy dog eyes he plants a tiny kiss on the corner of my mouth, as if he's afraid to kiss me full on when I'm pissed at him.

"I've been dealing with some shit and I didn't want to subject you to my bad mood, but I should have told you that instead of going radio silent."

I was geared up for some sort of conflict, but now he's taken the wind out of my sails. "Yes, you should have...Yeah. That."

He grins and I can't help but laugh. I shove at him before he envelopes me in his arms, smearing sweat all over my work blouse.

"You want to talk about it?" I ask, liking being held by him too much to complain about the sweat.

"I'd rather show you my bedroom," he says, burying his nose in my hair. "You smell fucking fantastic."

"Only because you smell so bad," I snark back.

"Maybe you should come help me shower?" For a guy who hasn't texted in two days he's pretty cocky.

I sigh. "And after that are we going to talk about what's been going on?"

He considers it for a moment, seeming to weigh the options. Luckily, he's twenty-four, so horny always wins. "Okay," he answers simply.

"Lead the way to the shower then," I tell him before he lifts me up and throws me over his shoulder, smacking me on the ass as we head to the master bath.

CHAPTER TWENTY-FOUR

Niko

ForeignXChange Group

Trish: I can't imagine a world without my best friend.

Twenty minutes in the shower with Tess does for me what forty-eight plus hours of booze, weights and pounding music hasn't. The sickening tension that's been under my skin since I left Christos at my parents' house two nights ago has finally subsided. But I know my newfound peace won't last long, so I'm relishing this interlude, lying in my bed, a naked Tess pressed to my side as I stroke her soft skin.

"I missed you," she whispers.

I kiss the top of her head where it rests on my chest. "I missed you too. I'm sorry I dropped out on you."

"It's okay, but don't do that again, okay?"

I nod, closing my eyes and taking a breath for what I know is coming next. She's a woman, there's no way she's not going to press this, and I can't blame her. I'd insist on it too if I were in her shoes.

"Are you ready to talk about it?" she asks.

No. I'm not ready to talk about it, and I'm particularly not ready to lie about it, which is exactly what I'm going to be forced to do in the next few minutes. I've thought it over and over, every angle I can look at, and there's no other option. No way to tell her my suspicions without getting her tangled in the whole mess, or risk consequences I can't even wrap my mind around.

"What do you want to know?" I answer her question with a question.

"What happened when you went to see Christos the other night?"

"We fought." It's the truth—not the details, I can't quite tell her all those—I'm determined that wherever I can, I'll tell her the truth.

"Oh-kay." She sighs. I'm not making this easy on her. "Can you elaborate?"

"He's either being a paranoid ass or he's keeping something from me, and I'm done with his shit. I told him so."

"He came to see me today," she says. My hand stops brushing along her ribcage and she pushes up, putting her chin on my chest so she can see my face.

"What did he want?" I'm afraid to hear the answer. I don't want to have to confront him again, but if he's harassing Tess I won't have a choice.

"To tell me that he was sorry for giving us such a hard time. And to make me promise that I won't hurt you."

I blink, my chest stinging painfully. "Why would he do that?" I ask, my voice gruff.

"I don't know, but I got the feeling there are things he wasn't telling me too."

She pauses, running a hand along my chest hair. I love when she touches me like this. I wish more than anything that we could shut out the rest of the world and spend all day touching each other. I don't think I'd ever tire of it.

"You aren't scared I'm going to do something to hurt you, are you?"

If she only knew that's the least of my worries. My greatest worry is what I might have to do that will hurt her. I hate this. All of it.

I sit up, bringing her with me so I can look at her and kiss her sweet lips. "No, baby. I know you'd never do anything to hurt me. I'm not sure what's going on with Christos, but it didn't come from me."

"I'm afraid your cousin might be a little whack, honey," she says, one eyebrow raised.

I chuckle and kiss her hard again before hopping out of bed. "You might be right." I grab a pair of sweats out of a drawer and put them on commando. "That's why I kicked his crazy ass out to the pool house. We've got the whole place to ourselves. Let's go eat something then work on christening some of the other rooms."

I spend the rest of the night trying to ignore the ache in my heart. I almost succeed.

**

My days take on a new pattern. In the mornings when Tess is at school I spend time digging around the various parts of Stephanos Shipping wherever I can. I have to be careful because if word gets back to my dad, he'll handcuff me—figuratively anyway. Christos and I are speaking, but only the bare essentials, whatever is necessary to get business done. He's moved to the operations division, and while my father asked about it, that's all he did. "I've heard you asked Christos to move?" he said. "Are you certain?" I assured him that I was and he simply nodded and left my office.

It was a sure sign that they truly are hiding something. My father would never have tolerated this from me otherwise. The three of us tiptoe around one another, no one willing to come out and say what's happened. I'm sure they're holding out hope that I haven't discovered their secret, and, of course, I'm digging in order to find out exactly what the secret is. But I know there is one. I can only hope that it's not as serious as I'm afraid it is.

I haven't gone back to my parents' house either. I've talked to my mother on the phone, but no church, no family dinners. My father has obviously told her something, because she's been remarkably low key about it.

This morning I've been in the records department scanning through months and months of previous shipping orders. I told the staff that I wanted to find a particular record but didn't know the name of the client, so I had to look for it myself. They didn't seem too stressed about it, so hopefully they won't mention it to my dad.

I'm sitting at a high-end computer in a spotless sterile room, the temperature kept at a nearly frigid eighteen Celsius. Massive servers are stored in here to keep all the company's records as far back as the beginning of my dad's tenure as CEO. Luckily, I worked in this section the summer after my senior year in high school, so I'm pretty familiar with the set up.

I'm not even sure what I'm looking for, but I know that it's got something to do with those crates of supposed medical supplies shipping from Los Angeles to Syria. I also suspect that it has something to do with the special accounts that Christos told Tess about. I wish like hell I hadn't been so distracted at the time, that I'd remembered to check into those, but I didn't, because, like a fool I thought that there couldn't possibly be anything off-color going on in my family's company. I trusted what I'd always been told about Stephanos Shipping, about who we were and what we stood for.

I scan dozens of files searching for an unfamiliar company name, a Los Angeles point of origin, anything with ties to Syria, but looking back six months I haven't found a single clue. Then, suddenly it's right in front of me. I've been so focused on the Los Angeles origination I didn't catch that Long Beach is listed. Shipments out of Long Beach, one a week for months. All going to Syria. *Fuck.*

I set the print parameters to give me a complete list of all the shipments that match that code and am sickened to find that they've been going on for nearly eighteen months. Once a month at first, then twice, now weekly. I carefully delete any records of my search, shut down the machine, and fold my printouts, stuffing them into the pocket of my jacket before I walk out of the records section, thanking the staff on my way, an easy smile pasted on my face.

I briskly make my way through the corridors of my company, the building where I grew up, the legacy that was promised to me from birth, and when I reach my office suite I tell Juliet that I'm not to be disturbed. This is why I've been doing my digging before Tess comes to work each day. I knew that if I did find something I couldn't face her immediately.

Going into my office, I close the door, locking it behind me. My hands are shaking as I take the printouts from my inside jacket pocket and open up the folded sheets to scan over the list of shipments. Pages and pages of them. From Long Beach to Syria. With no payments attached. And no indication that they actually stop here in Greece before heading out on a separate ship to complete the journey. It's a way to cover up a shipment.

The safe in my office is small, and honestly I've never had a reason to keep anything in it, but I'm quick to lock away these papers, and everything they might represent—the sullying of a respected Greek name, the destruction of an international success story. Once the tumblers click into place and the evidence is safe behind layers of impenetrable steel, I stride to the en suite bathroom, taking off my jacket as I go and dropping it on the floor. I step inside, kneel down on the marble tiles, and wrap my arms around the cold porcelain of the toilet as I vomit until every last bit of poison in my body has been expunged. And still I feel dirty.

I may never feel clean again.

CHAPTER TWENTY-FIVE

Tess

ForeignXChange Group

Tess: Are you guys taking geography at your schools?

When I arrive at work Niko is out. He's been doing that a lot lately. Annais said he's been scheduling all sorts of meetings outside the building. When I asked him about it he said he was tired of being cooped up inside and wanted a change of venue. I think he's still trying to avoid Christos.

He and I are fine, better than fine in certain ways, but overall our little world is not right. I can feel it, he can feel it, and still we don't talk about it. Last night I woke at two a.m. and I was alone in his bed. I went looking for him and found him sitting by the pool, staring at the water, a glass of ouzo in his hand. He looked so sad, so broken, all I could think to do was lie on the lounge chair with him, curling my body into his without a word, holding him.

He wrapped himself around me and clutched me as if I were the life raft that would keep him from drowning. I felt him shake as he buried his face in my hair, and I didn't say a word, both of us holding on—to what we don't know—until the sun rose over the island and we started another day of pretending.

**

Tuesdays are officially my least favorite day. My classes are difficult, I have to take notes for the senior accountants' planning meeting, and the I.T. staff have a consultant who comes in and uses my cubicle.

I walk out of the planning meeting and find that Nero, the consultant, has indeed arrived and co-opted my "office". I sigh, marching over and scooping my files and backpack off the corner of the desk so that I can find somewhere else to work.

"Sorry, girl," Nero says in his Indian-British accent. "I looked all over for another vacant desk, but the place is stuffed today." He smiles sheepishly. It's not his fault, but it's still irritating.

"It's okay. I'll go to the records office. It's cold in there, but I kind of like the hum of the servers."

He gives me a thumbs up and goes back to whatever crazy scrolling code he's working with. I haul my belongings down to the records office and stop off to check with the guy who runs the front desk.

"Hi, Kevin. Is it okay if I work in the server room? I need a computer to use, some consultant took mine."

Kevin looks up distractedly. "What is it, like, finance week down here or something?" he asks, clicking on various screens as he talks.

"What do you mean? Is someone else from finance here?"

"The CFO himself was down here all morning yesterday," he says, finally looking up at me. "You guys doing a special project?"

I'm puzzled, but I shake my head. "No. Just a coincidence I think."

I make my way to the back room and close the door behind me, setting all my things on the big table that holds the computers set up for researching company records. Normally staff only have access to the files that they're currently working on. Once a project is done or financial and shipping records are more than three months old, they're moved off of the active servers and put into the records.

As I log into the system and pull out my files to see which account I need to work on, I wonder what Niko was doing down here. He has minions, including me, to do research for him. A full-time secretary, a receptionist, an entire staff of people to find any information he could possibly desire. Why would he want to sit in this barren room with the company servers and do boring research?

I look through the list of accounts Annais gave me last week. I'm on my third batch of accounts since I first began the job, and I'm getting very familiar with the codes, which is why I immediately notice that I've got another of the special accounts with this batch. The mysterious codes sit at the end of the columns, mocking me, piquing my curiosity and annoying me at the same time.

I reach for the mouse to click on email and tell Christos that I have one of his special accounts. But as my cursor hovers over his address I'm overcome with the need to know exactly what these accounts actually are. Instead of the email I click on the icon for account records, quickly typing in the code for the special account.

A list of shipments pops up for some company with only initials—SKT, Inc. I scroll through the list, records that go back about a year and a half, the shipments gradually becoming more frequent. All of them are the same route, the same weight, the same number of containers, and the same contents—medical supplies. It's the route that catches my attention. The pick up is Long Beach, California, and the destination is the Syrian port of Lattakia. It makes sense to be sending medical supplies to Syria, which is torn to pieces by war, but the method, via water, makes no sense at all. Medical supplies are light enough to ship via air. Why would anyone ship something—especially medical supplies—over thousands of miles of ocean when they could fly it overland in half the time and probably at half the cost?

I'm curious as to how much it does cost to make those shipments. Working at Stephanos I've gotten a pretty decent idea of what things cost to ship certain distances. All I do is look at shipping charges and payments all day after all. This sounds expensive given what I know. Really expensive. I click on one of the shipments, going to the costs incurred line. It's blank, only another special code entered. I click on shipment after shipment and they're all the same—no costs incurred.

Warning bells are going off in my head now. I've completely forgotten about the work I was supposed to be doing today. I dig deeper and deeper into the accounts for SKT, Inc. I look up the company on the Internet and find nothing. I look for payments from them in our accruals records and come up empty-handed again. No costs incurred by them. No payments received from them. But shipments every week for months on end.

I should stop this, get back to my own work, tell Christos that he needs to pull that account from my caseload just like he told me to do. I should, but I can't. There are either procedures I don't know about, or something very bad is going on here. And for whatever reason, I don't trust Christos to tell me the truth. I could ask Niko, but what if I'm wrong and he's mad at me for digging around in his company's private records?

I sigh. In spite of my inner accountant telling me this is all very wrong, I can't cause more trouble for Niko right now. The last thing he needs is his student intern coming to him and making him search through company records, only to end up that this is some sort of special case. Maybe they're donating transport to an aid organization. Who knows what the real story is, but I need to stop and let it go.

So I do. I get back to work, and I put SKT, Inc. and mysterious shipments from California to Syria out of my head.

**

Niko and I are lying on the deck of his boat. The sun is warm, the waters are calm, and for the first time in weeks the real world seems miles away.

"Did I mention that this was an excellent idea on your part?" I ask.

"Once or twice," he answers, running a hand up and down my thigh as he kisses my belly button, slipping his tongue inside then flicking the gold ring that pierces the edge. Yes, Niko and I went on a rule-breaking binge yesterday. I got a belly button piercing, he got a tattoo. It's on the back of his shoulder and it's a beautiful sailboat—one of the old schooners with the multiple sails flying. Hot as hell.

I wiggle, the flutters in my tummy increasing the more he touches me. "I think we need to do this more often. I'm so happy I didn't have any papers to write this weekend."

Niko's hand slips inside my bikini top as his lips lower to mine. "Mmm. Thank God," he mumbles before kissing me. It's a long, languid kiss, seeming to go on for hours. I wrap my arms around him and sink into the feelings—warmth, protection, arousal. His hands skim my body, touching, testing, until one slides beneath the bottoms of my suit, his long fingers rubbing through the dampness of my core.

He growls. "Fuck, I love how wet you get," he tells me as he gently moves his first two fingers in and out of my channel.

I arch into him. "And I love how wet you make me," I breathe back. "Why don't—"

We jolt when we hear the ship's radio squawk from the cabin below. We both automatically hold our breath, listening for it to make more sounds. It does and I can't make out the words, but someone is talking, repeating a message several times.

"Probably the Coast Guard with some kind of general announcement," Niko tells me, standing. "Stay right here, I'll go see what it is."

He heads down the stairs and I can hear the radio, as well as the deep vibrations of his voice in response. After a couple of minutes there is silence, but Niko doesn't come back upstairs immediately. When he does his face is ashen, and his eyes don't meet mine.

"We need to head back," he says, his voice flat and his lips tense.

"What's happened?" I ask, standing and moving to him. Sensing that he needs my touch.

"Christos has been attacked again." He swallows, the whole thing physically distasteful to him. "He's unconscious. They're taking him in for emergency surgery." He looks at me, his eyes devastated. "His skull was crushed. He might not live."

**

The trip back to the island is fast, tight with tension, and silent. I work to get all of our things put back in order, throwing on my clothes over my swimsuit right away. The motor on the sailboat isn't meant to go fast, but it does the job well enough, and soon we're stepping off the deck onto the dock, almost running to Niko's car.

When we get to the hospital Niko agrees to let me take his car home with me and wait to hear from him. Eventually he'll need me, but right now he needs his family, and I know I'm right when he doesn't argue with me about it.

"Hey," I tell him before he runs into the ER doors. "He's strong. He's going to make it."

He gives me one hard kiss on the lips, and then he's gone.

I'm about to drive home when I remember that I left my backpack with all of my schoolwork at Niko's house. I turn the car the opposite direction and fifteen minutes later I pull into his brick driveway.

Inside the house is eerily quiet. The housekeeper is usually here this time of day, and I call out to her, but get no response. As I walk into the living room with its wall of glass that looks out over the pool, I notice the door to the pool house is wide open. Knowing Christos is in the hospital, I go outside to shut it and make sure his place is locked up while he's gone.

What I find when I reach the open doorway chills my blood and I cover my mouth with my hands to keep from screaming. My very first thought is that they might still be here—the bad guys, whoever did this to Christos. My heart races and I freeze, the urge to run strong, but fear holding me in place at the same time. Then rational thought sets in. Christos was brought to the hospital unconscious, someone must have found him here. Probably the housekeeper. All that commotion would have driven any bad guys away for sure.

I step into the small house, my ears straining to hear anything suspicious, my whole body sickened by the signs of what must have been a horrible struggle. It's like scars left on a place instead of a person, and it tells of Christos suffering something horribly violent.

Furniture is overturned, dishes are broken. The television set has been smashed to bits, and I see blood on the tile floor at the entrance to the kitchen. My stomach roils at the scene.

There are papers scattered everywhere, and the blood at the kitchen entrance smears across the floor and walls moving toward the bedroom. I can hear my parents' voices in my head, telling me not to touch anything—this is a crime scene, and I can't believe it's been left unattended like this. But in spite of knowing better, I walk further into the house, stunned by the wreckage that fills the small space.

I follow the blood smears until I get to the bedroom door. There, with a large hunting knife thrust into it, hangs a single sheet of paper. I step forward to read it and discover it's a shipping manifest. It's for a shipment that went out last week—from Long Beach to Syria, for SKT, Inc. The manifest lists seventy-two crates of medical supplies, but someone has used blood to circle that number—seventy-two. Then, with a dark pen they've written: *Where is number seventy-three, Ari? Bang. Bang. Your other boy's next.*

If I didn't know better I'd swear that ice crawls down my spine, spreading like a layer of frost over any warmth my body held until this moment. I struggle to swallow, my throat swollen in horror. I press back against the wall struggling to sift through the overload of information I'm ingesting.

Your other boy. Niko. They're talking about Niko. He's next. "Nooo," the sound pushes out of my throat like someone squeezed me too hard, crushing my ribs, my lungs, my essence leaking out along with the sound. Not Niko. They can't hurt Niko. But in the back of my mind other things are tumbling around like slippery marbles, as I fight to grasp even just one and examine it.

Long Beach to Syria. Where is number seventy-three? Bang. Bang. The world grinds to a halt and I stare, wide-eyes filled with tears. Drugs? No. Syria. A warzone. Bang. Bang. Guns. Over sea not air. No record of money for the shipments. Special accounts that only Christos should work on.

In that moment I realize that at least some of Ari Stephanos's billions are coming from helping terrorists run guns to factions in warring Syria.

I slide down the wall, the totality of what's happening sweeping over me in broad strokes, each back and forth showing me another consequence. Niko in danger. Niko in jail. Christos in a coma. My career ruined. Stephanos Shipping destroyed. CIA, FBI, International courts, prosecution in multiple countries. "God, no," I cry to the empty house. "No, no, no." My sobs are loud and fast. I bring my knees to my chest, and drop my head to them; huge, choking, gasping sobs spilling out along with the tears.

And in the midst of it all I see Niko, lying on his boat, golden skin exposed, a happy smile on his lips, one hand stretched out over my stomach possessively.

"No, no, no," I repeat, my voice now hoarse and broken. Who knew that paradise could turn to hell in the time it takes to read twelve words. Twelve words that have changed my entire world, and Niko's too.

CHAPTER TWENTY-SIX

Niko

ForeignXChange Group

Darla: I'm so sick. I thought for sure going to the hookah bar last night would help, but I still feel like I'm going to die.

I've been in the hospital waiting room for hours. My parents and Christos's are in a private room down the hall, but I've exiled myself to this public one. I don't deserve to be part of Christos's inner circle right now. I left him when I knew he was in over his head, and now he may not survive it.

I've tried to ask my father what happened and all he'd say was, "Later," but I can tell he knows. He knows who did this to Christos and he's heart sick about it.

Once we're out of the hospital I'm done with this bullshit though. He *will* tell me what they've done and why they did it, and then we're going to figure out how to *un*do it. I'm going to fight to save my family's company with everything I've got. I just need a little more time to figure it all out.

I'm leaned back in a chair deleting emails off of my phone when the text from Tess comes in.

Can you meet me in the lobby?

I quickly type back *yes*, and make my way to the elevators. During the trip down I wonder what's happened. She knows I'll get in touch as soon as I have any news. I hope she hasn't had trouble with my car. Now I'm trying to decide how I'll handle it if she tells me she scratched my prize possession. I repeat the mantra, *you love Tess*, over and over a few times to prepare.

When I exit the elevator she's standing a few feet away, her back to me as she looks out the windows of the lobby.

"Hey," I put a hand on her shoulder as I walk up, "what's going on?"

When she turns to look at me I know immediately that something far more valuable than my car is broken. Her face is a study in devastation, her eyes swollen, her cheeks red, and track marks from the tears still drying on her soft skin.

"What happened?" I implore, looking at her eyes trying to discern if she's been hurt by someone. What if the guys who got to Christos found Tess? "God, are you okay?" My heart races and I can't help but look down to see if she's bruised, if her clothes are torn. The possibilities ricocheting through my overworked mind are horrifying.

"Can we take a walk?" she asks, pulling away from me and not looking me in the eyes. Fuck. This is bad. Really bad.

I nod, swallowing around my dry throat, and she leads me out the front doors to the small garden space adjacent to the building.

As soon as we step into the path through the garden she turns to face me. I see her eyes dart over my shoulder before she begins talking.

"I went to your house. Christos must have been attacked in the pool house." She bites her lip, trying to control the tears that well up in her eyes. Jesus. She must have been scared senseless.

"God, baby." I pull her to me, wrapping my arms around her, but she keeps hers crossed, a barrier between her body and mine, so I release her.

"The place is trashed, he must have fought them hard."

My chest shudders as I try to remember to breathe.

"They left a note," she continues.

My heart stops. "What?" I ask, everything inside of me tightening in reaction.

She pulls out a piece of paper from her purse, holding it with her shirtsleeve pulled over her hand. It has blood smeared on it, and as she holds it in front of me I reach out to take it, but she stops me. "Don't touch it. It's evidence and you can't get your fingerprints on it."

I nod, but not really processing what she means. I look at the scrap, trying not to gag at the metallic smell of the fresh blood that mars the white of the paper. As soon as I see the *shipment destination* in the third column I know what it is—Syria. I read the words scrawled above the *units shipped* and a burning starts behind my eyes. The last time I cried was when my grandmother died my senior year in college. I won't give in now, because I will not give these people the valuable commodity that are my tears. I save them for people and things that I love.

When I speak, my voice is hoarse and dead. "You can't take this to the police, Tess."

"Did you know?" she asks, and I realize that she understands all too well what that piece of paper means. But how?

"Did I know what?" I ask carefully.

"That your dad was running guns for some sort of terrorist group?"

The pain nearly doubles me over. If my father had taken a knife to my soft center he couldn't have gutted me any cleaner.

"Why would you think he is?" I ask, the defensiveness in my tone catching even me off-guard.

She shakes her head, putting the piece of paper back in her bag. Her eyes are so sad I might die from the urge to touch her, comfort her, but I can't, because I think I'm about to lose Tess for good.

"Don't pretend with me, Niko. We've never lied to each other. At least I didn't think we had. I've seen the records of the shipments from Long Beach to Syria, and all those 'special accounts' that Christos didn't want me to work on. Now the assaults and the threats. Your dad's involved with someone very dangerous, and what I want…no. What I *need* to find out is did you know?"

I sit down on a nearby bench, my body suddenly so heavy I don't think I can support it another moment. I put my head in my hands before looking up at her, the most beautiful girl I've ever known. The rule follower who's about to become my family's worst enemy.

"I didn't know anything until the first time Christos was attacked." I sigh, elbows on my knees as I look at the concrete below me. "That night I overheard him and my dad talking—he said he'd been attacked by someone speaking Arabic and my dad said he needed to handle the shipments personally from then on. I could tell it wasn't standard business but I didn't know exactly what was happening."

She nods to indicate I should continue. I briefly wonder how far she'll go. Will she tell them about this conversation? The FBI, the CIA? Will I end up in prison too?

"I've been looking into it, trying to figure out what shipments were coming out of Los Angeles." I pause. "I also saw suspicious crates at the loading docks. And things being loaded onto tankers that shouldn't have been. They must have been bringing the stuff here and then putting it on different ships to get it to Syria."

"When did you figure it out?" she asks softly.

"I hadn't entirely. Is it…is it guns?"

She nods. "It has to be."

"Fuck," I whisper.

"Yeah," she chuckles bitterly.

"Tess. You can't—"

She cuts me off. "Can't *what*?" She's angry now, tears streaming down her face. "Can't tell? Can't let anyone know? Do you want me to burn this note then? Or maybe give it to your dad so he can see that he's in some sort of war with the scariest guys on the planet?" She laughs and it's almost maniacal. She's about to break down, but so am I.

"Don't make me choose, Niko." Her voice breaks.

"Don't make *me*," I snap back, regretting it nearly the second the words leave my mouth.

She stares at me, all of her heartbreak written on her beautiful face, and I feel like a train is barreling down on me in the dark of night and there's no place to go, nowhere safe to jump. It's going to tear into me no matter what, and all I can do is watch it happen.

"Tess," my voice is softer now. "It's my family."

"And it's who I *am*," she answers. "It could ruin my career. I could end up in jail. It violates every single value and ideal I've had my entire life."

And in that brief moment I realize what Christos was so afraid of. What he's feared ever since he first found out who Tess's family is. He's been afraid of this. This moment when she would choose her family— the law—over me.

"I love you," I whisper.

"And would you still if I weren't who I am?" she asks.

I look at her, and I know she's right. I know that her integrity is one of the things that drew me to her in the first place. The strength of her convictions, the way she conducted herself. She's one of the most valiant people I've ever known, and I love her for that.

"I don't know," I answer honestly. "All I do know is that I can't sit by and let my dad and Christos go to prison."

She nods. "I understand." Then she takes a deep breath and dries her tears. "You do what you have to do, Niko. But I'll do the same."

She turns slowly and starts to walk away, and it takes everything I've got not to leap up and tear after her. My heart is screaming for her to stop, my head is railing in protest. My legs are jonesing to follow her one last time.

"Tess," I say roughly before she reaches the parking lot.

She turns and watches me, warily, and I know that it's already happened. She's left me, and now I'm the enemy.

"I'll never forget you," I say.

"I know I'm going to *wish* I could forget you," she answers before she walks away.

CHAPTER TWENTY-SEVEN

Tess

ForeignXChange Group

Tess: I think sometimes you have to let your body rest.

"How long are you going to sit there thinking about it?" Cass asks gently from the doorway of our bedroom.

I look up from my place on the bed where I've been staring at the phone for hours. I need to call the police. I need to tell them to investigate the crime scene at Niko's house. I need to turn over the letter from the guys who attacked Christos. I need to turn Niko's family into the authorities. They've been helping to run illegal weapons for terrorists. They've violated all kinds of laws I don't even know about. Greek laws, international laws, US laws. It's not a coincidence that Nate's been warning me about them since I got here. He knew something wasn't right, even if he might not have known the specifics.

Yes, I need to call the police.

"Tess?" Cass says again. I look at her and it's like I'm watching her through a tunnel. She's far away and not quite real. Not quite physically here with me.

"Yeah," I say, staring at her as if she's an attraction at a zoo.

She walks over and sits next to me, grabbing ahold of my hand. "You need to do this. You can't risk getting implicated in the whole thing. This is going to be huge, and once everyone knows you've been dating Niko they're going to come after you, thinking you know things. And you do, right? You know things?"

I told Cass the basics of what was happening, but I didn't want to give her any specific information so that she wouldn't be trapped in this the way I am. I now have a legal obligation to tell the authorities what I know—things that will set the wheels in motion. Things that will destroy Niko and his family.

Truthfully, I imagine it's all going to come out very soon no matter what I do, but I can speed up the process if I tell. And I have this damn letter. Smeared with what I'm sure is Christos's blood.

"Tess, you're scaring me," Cass says. She runs a hand over my hair, like you would a small child. And I feel small. Too small for this weight. Too young for this responsibility. Too sad for this task.

"I'll be okay," I tell her, my voice hardly more than a whisper. "I just need a few more minutes alone. To collect my thoughts. Decide exactly what I'm going to say. Okay?" I give her a weak smile and she continues to give me the furrowed brow Cass-is-concerned look.

"Okay. I'm going to go get some dinner started, Anton's bringing you some of that wine you like so much and we're all going to eat and watch Lord of the Rings. So get this call out of the way so you can relax with us tonight. Promise me."

I nod my head. "I promise. Just a few more minutes."

She stands, her expression telling me that if I don't do this in the next few minutes things are going to get ugly. She's a lot bigger than me, so I probably shouldn't test her resolve.

"See you in the kitchen in a bit," she says before leaving the room, shutting the door softly behind her.

When I was a teenager I once asked my mother how she'd known that my dad was "the one" for her.

She was standing in our kitchen at the house I grew up in, the house my parents still live in. I was propped up on a barstool at the counter where she served Nate and I hundreds of meals over the course of our childhoods. I used to eat at that counter, do my homework at that counter, and that day I listened to secrets of my mother's heart at that counter.

She paused to think, but then went back to wiping down the countertops, her hands always moving, scrubbing, sorting, organizing—the same way she did with all of our lives. She was the hub of our family wheel, and she managed and directed us like a general with her troops.

"First of all," she said, winking at me, "you have to believe that there is a 'one'. Some people don't. But I always did. Even when I had bad date after bad date, and got my heart stomped on by all kinds of men, I always believed that there was that one guy out there who was meant for me.

"But how did I know that your dad was that guy I'd been waiting for? I could say it was because things were simpler with him than with other guys, but they weren't necessarily. His complications were things I didn't mind as much as other people's complications, but that didn't mean he didn't have any. We all do."

She handed me a glass of water even though I hadn't asked for one—yet. Mothers are weird that way.

"I could also say that it was because he put me first no matter what. But honestly, love, no one can put someone else first always—in the big picture yes, but not all day every day. Life is hard, people have obligations and responsibilities. There were plenty of times that your dad had to put a meeting or a project ahead of my birthday or your swim meet. Our jobs pay for the house and the food, and sometimes that has to come before any grand gestures to our partners."

By now I was focused on her like a laser, waiting for the magic pearl that was going to give me the secrets to one of the universe's great mysteries.

"I think the way you know that you've found your one is when you realize that you are the best version of yourself when you're with him." She nodded as if agreeing with her own interpretation.

"When you first meet a new boy, it's so easy to adjust yourself to suit him. It's natural. We all try to be our best, shiniest selves for that person we're infatuated with. But, once that wears off, who are you? Are you a person pretending to like camping because he does? Are you petty and jealous because he makes you insecure? Are you worried about your weight because his last girlfriend was two sizes smaller than you?

"Or, are you *more* confident because he helps you believe you can do anything you set out to do? Do you feel beautiful because you know he thinks you are? Can you see your weaknesses only because he helps you learn to overcome them? Your dad did all those things for me," she said. "He does all those things for me everyday. He helps make me be the best person I can be. That's how I knew he was the *one*. I'm better with him than I was without him."

My eyes fill as I remember her words that day, and I think back to the moments I had with Niko. The way he understood my commitment to right and wrong, but still challenged me to look at things in a different way. The way he made me feel like I was the most beautiful thing he'd ever seen. The way he placed total confidence in me at work, and total faith in me outside of work.

Niko made me a better person. Someone who can consider the good and the bad of things, and make judgments that are based on the particulars of a circumstance, rather than blindly following rules. Rules need to be followed, but they need to be understood too. We need to assess our rules just as we would anything else in our lives. Otherwise we can end up with rules that are bad or worthless, or even dangerous, and we can follow them straight to our own demise. Rules are, after all, made by humans, and we are flawed, fallible creatures.

Kind of like Ari Stephanos is flawed and fallible. His love for his son and his company are apparent. He's a kind man who made a horrible mistake. Why, I might never know, but I've learned enough from my time with

Niko to realize that there is a story there that matters just as much as the laws that he broke.

Niko taught me a lot over the last few weeks, and when my heart reminds my brain of that I have to admit—I'm a better person with Niko than I was without him.

I think Niko Stephanos might have been my one.

The realization cleaves my poor bruised heart clean in two, and I shudder at the brutal reality of what's happened today. I've lost him. My one. And now I will never get him back.

But, even if I can't *have* him, I can *save* him. And I know now that I have to. For the man who cared enough to make me a better person, I will give him a better chance—a better chance at life, a better chance at surviving this. Because sometimes you have to bend some rules for the ones you love.

CHAPTER TWENTY-EIGHT

Niko

ForeignXChange Group

Kellie: And I thought the bomb *made a mess.*

The sounds of broken glass being swept across terra cotta tiles reach me in my bedroom where I sit in the darkness looking out over the pool, while workmen clean away the evidence of the attack on Christos.

I wrap my fingers around the tumbler of scotch in my right hand before I raise it to my lips and tilt my head back, letting the warm liquid flow down my throat, relishing the burn that follows in its wake.

There are guards everywhere now. Here on Georgios where my family once thought we'd always be safe. They stand outside every door to my house, they stand outside Christos's hospital room, they guard my sisters in their homes, and they will follow every one of my nieces and nephews to school and back tomorrow…and the next day…and the next.

I breathe deeply, trying to quell the hot, oozing anger that sits inside my chest. It threatens to bubble up and lay waste to everything in its path. My father—Ari to me now—has told me the whole story. How the company began to fail, how he was too proud to speak of it with anyone and instead took loans from terrorists. How they offered him only one way to pay back the money—run guns to the Middle East.

My heart died a little more when he told me that he let Christos in on it, because he didn't want me tainted. His perfect boy. His golden heir. He tried to keep me pure by sullying my best friend, his own nephew, my deftheri. And like the good soldier he is, Christos took it on. Communicating with the terrorists, figuring out a way to circumvent our accounting systems with special codes and secret records. But then a shipment went awry. The Somalian pirates took one of our ships and two dozen crates of MK-17s. And the terrorists went after Christos as a warning. Then it happened again. And they came after Christos harder.

And Christos knew what was coming. It's why he was so inexplicably paranoid about Tess. The sister of an FBI agent, the daughter of a district attorney. Christos knew that she was too close, and once she found out, she'd turn Stephanos Shipping in. But even if Tess wasn't going straight to the officials this evening, I think Ari would be caught in the not so distant future. The inquiries by the IRS, the piracy off the Somalian coast—the warnings were there, and my guess is the charges won't be far behind.

That's why I didn't tell Ari that Tess knew. I can't stand the idea that my family could blame her for whatever happens. I left him sitting in the hospital, waiting to see if the nephew he sentenced to this will survive. I told him that I'm in charge of the family now, and he didn't say a word.

I've thought through every possible angle over the last few hours, and I know that I can't save the company. They'll freeze assets, bust down doors, strip computer files. It will be chaos, and it will go on for a very long time. Lawyers and trials and international negotiations. I have no idea how it will all play out, but I know that it will be brutal and complex, and lengthy.

I have two choices now—sit and wait, or save who I can. While it breaks my heart to imagine my father in a prison cell for the remainder of his days, I cannot worry about him. He made his bed, and now he'll have to sleep in it. Ari Stephanos was a great man, but he will be remembered as a tragic one, and I know that I'll have to deal with my feelings about him at some point, but I can't afford the distraction now.

This evening I transferred every dime I could from my father's accounts to a trust at a Swiss bank set up in my oldest sister's name. She isn't employed by Stephanos, isn't married to a Stephanos employee, and won't be part of this investigation. She will be in charge of supporting my mother and other sisters when Ari's assets are taken and he's left penniless. My grandparents have always lived on their own investments and they own their house outright, I don't think even the world's most cunning lawyers will go after an eighty-year-old man and his equally ancient wife. I only wish I could save them from the heartbreak they will suffer when they find out what their son has done to the family legacy.

With my mother and sisters protected, I can focus on saving Christos. They don't know if he'll survive his injuries, but I have to believe he will. I have to believe that the guy I've loved all my life isn't lost to me forever. And I have to insure that when he does wake up he's not faced with a life in prison.

Legally, Christos is well past the age when he could be excused for his actions. But I know that he shouldn't be punished for them either. He did what should have been my job, took the risk for me, sacrificed himself so that I would be innocent, and for that I owe him. I may never understand why he was willing to cooperate with my father's mistakes, but loyalty gone awry is still loyalty. And I share over twenty years of brotherhood with this man who would actually take a bullet for me. I can't let him be pulled under with Ari. I have to fight to save him.

I take one last slug of the scotch and set the glass down on the end table next to me. As I stand, I see that the sun is rising and the edges of the sky have turned pink and gold. It reminds me of Tess, her gold hair and pink cheeks, and I have to lean against a nearby dresser for a moment in order to breathe through the wave of pain that crashes into me. It's physically exhausting, thinking of a life without her in it, but even if she had stayed I have nothing left to offer her. I'm no longer Niko Stephanos. I'm not sure who I'll be after today, and I'd never subject her to that. She deserves someone's best. My best is probably long gone.

**

I'm surprised that the police station is as quiet as it is. Even though it's early, I'd expected to see cars, maybe some journalists, Greek Intelligence. But when I walk in there is only one desk clerk here, and the hum of the soda machine in the lobby.

"Hi," I say to get the clerk's attention. He stands and walks over, his face breaking into a smile when he recognizes me.

"Good morning Mr. Stephanos. I hope it's not something bad that's brought you by?"

I'd think that the guy is fucking with me, but he seems genuinely clueless about why I'm here.

"I'd like to see the Commander please," I say, not willing to give anything away.

"Certainly," he answers.

Five long minutes later I'm seated in front of the desk of the island's police commander.

"What can I do for you, Mr. Stephanos?"

I look at him—the relaxed posture, the genuine smile. This is either one of the world's great actors or a man who hasn't heard that my family has been helping the terrorists run weapons to Syria.

And if he doesn't know, that means Tess didn't tell him. And maybe that means Tess didn't tell anyone. Maybe she never will. My heart thuds hard in my chest—twice. Then it flutters the tiniest bit as well. Like a butterfly that's been knocked senseless, only to move its wings again for a brief second of hope. But I can't hope. I have no right to hope. Whether Tess turns Ari in or not, I'm not worthy of her anymore. Someone with Tess's integrity could never be happy with a man who is willing to break the kinds of rules I am. Tess lives her beliefs. I've lost the luxury of that now.

"Commander," I begin, tucking that stupid fluttering heart away for good, "I have information about a very serious crime that's been committed on the island, a crime of international significance, and I'm responsible for all of it."

CHAPTER TWENTY-NINE

Tess

ForeignXChange Group

Tess: I have to go home you guys. I guess that means this is it. Antio (at least I learned how to say goodbye in Greek).

"She can give you plenty of information about the accounting system, she's a goddamn accountant, but not if you won't provide the immunity," my father yells, banging his fist on the table in front of him. We've been locked in a hotel conference room in Athens for two days, and while I'm sure he's tired, I know that this is part of the act. He and the team he flew here—a hotshot international law specialist from New York, and a criminal defense attorney from

Athens—have been hammering out a deal with the Greek Intelligence agents as well as the CIA and FBI. Nate flew in separate from my dad, but he's been here the whole time as well.

"You understand that we've already offered immunity to the nephew, if we give it to the son as well that leaves us with Ari Stephanos as the sole family member responsible for this mess," the leader of the Greek contingent complains.

"As it should be," my father responds. "Those young men have absolutely no criminal background and the son in particular never participated in any of the transactions as far as we can tell."

"Then why did he confess?"

My father sighs, shaking his head. "Because he's protecting the rest of his family. Does that really surprise you?"

"Even if that is true, he was the fucking CFO," the other man answers, "it all happened on his watch, you know we could make a case with that."

"Incompetence isn't guilt," my dad's New York buddy snarks. It hurts me to hear Niko disparaged like that. He wasn't incompetent, he was coddled, led to believe that his family would never lead him astray. Conditioned for twenty-four years to trust them absolutely. But I keep my thoughts to myself, even though it's hard not to rise to his defense.

My brother looks at me sympathetically. I know he can tell what's going through my mind.

"Look," my dad says, "Ari's the big fish. What we're going to hand you is enough evidence to insure that you have an airtight case. You'll put him away for life, you'll get a very nice addition to the government's coffers when you confiscate all of his assets, and the international intelligence community will get some valuable intel on the group he was in debt to. So the two kids get off—and then what? The family will be without resources, the company will be defunct. They're going to suffer plenty."

The Greek guys all look at one another, and finally the leader nods his head. "All right. Since the CIA and FBI have agreed to the same in their prosecutions, we'll sign."

A sigh of relief presses out of every person in the room. My dad stands and puts his hand out across the table to the Greeks, who all shake it. Then the other attorneys do the same—everyone shakes with everyone and seems to be pleased with the deal. The papers are edited, reprinted, and signed, and for the first time in days I feel as though I can breathe. Niko is safe, and that's all that matters to me.

**

"Still can't get ahold of him?" Nate asks as he enters our hotel suite and heads to the mini-fridge, pulling out a beer and popping the top.

I shake my head. I know it's ridiculous to keep trying, but in another few hours it'll all be moot, so I keep hoping. Once I set foot on that airplane I have to let him go though. I know this.

"He's got a lot on his plate right now, Mess," Nate says kindly, sitting down next to me on the sofa. "Maybe in a few months after some of this shit has settled down you can try again."

I wipe away the tear that's snuck out of my eye. "No, it's over. All this—" I wave my arm around the hotel room as if it represents the disaster of Ari's criminal endeavors, "—is too much to overcome. I don't blame him, I said I'd turn him in, and even though I tried to save him at the same time, how can you get over something like that?"

"Aw Mess." Nate wraps an arm around me and I lay my head on his shoulder, sniffing. "You're only twenty-one years old and you were faced with an impossible situation. You did a good thing. You called Dad and me, you worked with the law, and you ended up saving a guy who was innocent. I know your heart hurts, but your head should be proud. Dad and I are both really proud of you."

"Thanks, Nate."

"Anytime. I'm just sorry that you won't get to finish up your exchange year."

"It's okay. Study abroad has sort of lost its luster." We both laugh at the understatement.

"But Mess?"

"Yeah?"

"Promise me you'll be ready next time."

I look at him quizzically.

"Next time some guy comes around—someone you could really be into. Don't let this make you bitter or scared. You've never been scared of anything and I don't want to see you change."

I give him a small smile. My heart wants to protest, tell him that there won't be a next time, that Niko is it for me, my one. I can't possibly consider the possibility that I might meet someone who would take his place. But I don't want to upset Nate, and I also know that at twenty-one years old I'd be a fool to discount the possibility. I also know that it will be a very long time before I can even consider that possibility. My heart belongs to Niko, and I have a feeling that a part of it will forever.

But that's not what my big brother, who's already worried about me, wants to hear.

"I'll be ready," I say. "But for now, I just want to go home."

"Sounds good. I'll see if Dad's ready to call the taxi."

"Thank you, Nate. You really are a good brother."

"You're welcome, Mess. I love you."

"Love you too."

Six Months Later

I'm standing at the dock, the wind whipping my hair around my head. It's spring in Chicago, and while the day is pretty warm, the wind isn't. I huddle into my faux shearling jacket and wonder again why the hell Nate insisted I meet him here. It's not like he takes a boat to get to town.

But he was very specific, he said I had to stand at this dock, at this time, and that he had a surprise for me. The only thing I can guess is he's taken up with a girl at one of the tour companies or he bought a boat. Although why in the world he'd keep a boat here when he lives in D.C. I have no idea.

There are about six ships disembarking and boarding here right now. Tour boats, big ships that cruise the harbor with loads of tourists. I hope that Nate can find me, because at my height I can't see jack around all these people. Some huge guy pushing a stroller with three kids hanging off of it knocks into me as he passes by, and before I know it I'm flying, feet off the ground, pitching forward, about to crash headlong into someone's back, when I get jerked upright again, a pair of very strong hands grasping my shoulders.

"Are you okay?" a deep voice says in my ear. My entire body tenses, my heart kicking up to record-breaking levels.

I slowly turn, until I'm facing a broad chest covered in a tight blue t-shirt, pecs and abs peeking through the thin cotton. My eyes travel upward, and I'm having a hard time catching my breath, because deep down I know what I'm going to see when the journey's done— the most beautiful pair of blue eyes God ever put on a man.

"Oh," I gasp as I look at him.

Niko gives me a smile and I'm stunned, any coherent thoughts blown right out of my head.

"Tess," he whispers, his gaze flicking from my eyes to my mouth and back again.

"What are you doing here?" I ask, my voice ridiculously breathy.

His hands travel slowly down my arms and back up again. I wet my lips and I see his eyes go dark.

"I came for you," he says.

"Uh." I'm speechless.

"Can we talk? For a few minutes?"

"Okay," I whisper. Apparently my voice has taken a hiatus.

He grasps my hand and we start to walk through the crowds back toward the boardwalk.

Suddenly I remember Nate. "Wait! My brother. I was supposed to meet my brother here," I tell him, my heart plummeting inside my chest. What if Niko thinks I don't want to talk to him and leaves now?

"He's not coming, princess," he says, grinning.

"What? How do you...it was *you* the whole time? You I was supposed to meet here today? *You're* the surprise?"

He nods. "Nate and I have been talking for the last few months. I finally convinced him I was an okay guy so he did me a solid."

I shake my head and roll my eyes. Nate will be hearing from me about his meddling, but for now I want to hear what Niko has to tell me.

He pulls me behind him again and we continue along the waterfront passing boat slips until I see a familiar sight—Niko's sailboat. "You brought your boat," I say.

"Same model, but a different boat," he tells me as we approach.

I look at it, trying to catalogue the differences. The deck is a different kind of wood, and there's a stripe along the side. Then my eyes stop at the name written across the bow. *Tess*, it says in large dark blue and gold letters.

I stop, looking at the name and trying not to fall apart. He named his boat after me. I think I might die.

He stands behind me, his big body hot and far too close. "You see the name?" he whispers in my ear as he leans down, his lips brushing against my hair. I hear him make a small sound deep in his chest and everything inside of me collapses, a quivering pile of jello.

"Come aboard?" he asks.

I nod, nearly choking on the hope that's swelling inside me.

Once we're on board, Niko offers to make me a coffee to help warm up. I accept the offer and wait on deck while he goes below to the espresso maker. My mind is reeling from seeing him, touching him, having him here in my hometown, on a boat with my name painted on the side.

I look around the familiar structure of the boat, remembering each time we laid on the deck, made love, kissed, talked, dreamed. I've worked so hard not to have those memories, they're almost as painful as if they happened yesterday.

That's why when he comes back upstairs, carrying two demitasse cups of espresso, I'm standing in the middle of the deck crying like a snot-nosed freak.

He sets the cups down on the bench along the edge of the deck and pulls me into his arms. "What's wrong, princess? Should I not have come?"

I bury my face in his chest for a moment, smelling his familiar scent—the ocean, and soap and that special something that's all him.

I shake my head, getting his t-shirt wet in the process. When I lift my head to look at him his lips are so close my breath catches in my chest.

"Tess," he whispers. "I missed you so much."

"I missed you too," I answer, my voice hoarse with want.

"I have so much to tell you."

"We should talk," I agree.

"Can we do this first?" he asks, as he lowers his head and brushes his lips across mine. I can't control the moan that falls from my chest. His lips make another pass over mine, and I press against him, desire flaring to life in an instant.

My tongue slips out to wet my lips and he growls, cupping the back of my head and crushing his mouth to mine. Our tongues intertwine, and we perform a choreography that's familiar yet tantalizingly new.

Our breath comes fast, and our bodies arch against one another, both of us craving something so near yet so far. I stroke his stubbly cheek with my palm, my other hand finding the silky hair at the nape of his neck. It's longer than it used to be, and I relish the soft curls.

"Tess," he gasps, pulling away and giving me a series of small kisses along my jaw. "We need to talk." When did he become the voice of reason?

I pull back, tucking my hands back into my jacket pockets. "Okay. You're right."

He smiles at me, but it's strained, and I can't help but notice that he adjusts his jeans surreptitiously as we walk to the bench and pick up our espressos.

"This is perfect," I say as I take my first sip.

"I remember how you like it," he says, shrugging.

We both pause and sip some more.

"So are you going to tell me what you're doing here?"

"Yeah, princess," he says, a warm smile on his face. "I am."

CHAPTER THIRTY

Niko

ForeignXChange Group

Paisely: We do have a Degas at the Hermitage, Tess. It's called L'etoile, and it is a beautiful ballerina onstage, face upturned, arms outspread, flowers drifting down from her skirts. She is hope and youth and rebirth, and like the title of the painting, she is the star of her own life.

Tess is more beautiful than even my memory made her. Her blonde hair is floating around her face in the slight breeze that blows up off the lake, and her big blue eyes gaze at me, so open and genuine it's like I can see into her soul.

"I'm not sure where to start," I say, looking out over the water. "I guess from the beginning."

She nods, encouraging me to spill some of the hardest months of my life.

I'm Greek, and I come from a culture known first and foremost for its great storytelling, so I decide to tell Tess a story—the story of me.

"After you left," I begin, "I went and turned myself in, hoping to take the blame so that Christos wouldn't go to prison."

She looks at me and tears well up in her eyes. "I know," she whispers.

I smile. "But some stubborn woman I know wouldn't let that happen. How can I ever thank you for what you did for me and for Christos? I've spoken to your brother and your dad several times, but I didn't want to approach you until my life was under control."

She nods. She gets it. She's always understood me, even when I wasn't so sure about myself.

"After they released me and told me about the deal that your dad negotiated, they brought formal charges against Ari." I still can't bring myself to call him Dad. We talk when we can, and my mother pushes at me to be more forgiving, but the man destroyed everything that mattered to me in this world, and I'm not sure when I'll be able to see him without seeing that too.

"There were a lot of times when I didn't leave the office for days. My uncle and I had to be on site to assist the officials while they went through the company records. At the same time, agents were at my mother's house going through papers and computers, confiscating assets. We had to cancel most of our standing shipments, and dock the ships in Athens and

Miami." Most of those ships have been auctioned off now, the proceeds used to pay fines in the US and Greece.

"What about Christos?" Tess asks. "Is he…is he okay?"

I sigh. There's still not a day that goes by when I don't miss him.

"He's okay. I mean, he's recovered almost entirely. He'll always have some hearing loss in one ear, and his right hand has some loss of function, but you'd never know any of it by looking at him. He got so lucky, Tess."

"I'm glad. I'm really glad. He never deserved any of that."

I nod. "He can't work at Stephanos anymore, the government wouldn't allow it, so he had to come up with something else to do with his life. You'll never believe this, but he wants to go to medical school."

"Really?" she asks, sounding as surprised as I felt the first time I heard.

"Yeah. All that time in the hospital I guess."

"Good for him though."

"Yeah. I'm really proud of him. We talk every couple of weeks. He's living at his family's place in Athens and getting ready to apply to med school there."

"Your mom and your sisters?" she asks.

"They're fine. I—" I stop, realizing that I shouldn't put Tess in the position of knowing that I hid funds to support my mom before the officials could freeze all of our accounts. "Let's just say I made sure they're taken care of—always. And my uncle is watching out for them."

"Your dad's still waiting for trial?"

"Yeah. It'll be months. They've got him in a decent place though. He seems okay. Hasn't lost too much weight. The other inmates are white collar too, so there isn't any physical danger." Talking about my father in prison might be one of my least favorite things in the world, but I'm getting used to it bit by bit.

"And you?" she finally asks. "Tell me about my favorite member of the Stephanos family."

I smile. "After the company got settled and my uncle had everything under control, I knew it was time to figure out my own shit. I had two things I was good at," I tell her. "Ships and business."

"So you're doing something with both I'm guessing," she says, a big smile breaking out across her beautiful face.

"I am. I started a company in Miami, sailing tours and lessons. I've got two ships there—the boat I brought from Greece that we give lessons on, and a schooner for tours. You should see her, she's beautiful."

I've been nervous to tell Tess this. When she met me I was a billionaire, the CFO of an international corporation. Now I've got a nice sized trust fund that the government agreed to leave alone, and a great start to a business, but my situation in the world is very different than it once was.

But when I look at her now, as I explain my business to her, all I see in her eyes is pride, and it lights a fire inside of me that makes me want to work more hours, try harder, do bigger and better things every day. If she were with me, I'd work my ass off seven days a week to put that look on her face.

"Why Miami?" she asks.

"I needed a fresh start, you know? Everyone at home—they were good to us. I know my mom and sisters will be well taken care of on the island, but I needed to be somewhere I could be me, not Ari's son.

"I went to Miami first because I knew it, I'd lived there before, had some old contacts, and I wanted to get my feet on solid ground before I expanded to phase two of my plan."

Her eyes get bigger and her tongue darts out of her mouth for a moment, wetting her lips. It distracts me, but I force myself to get back on track.

"I'm hoping to open a second location...here in Chicago." I wait, my heart about to burst out of my chest.

"Here?" she asks, breathless.

"Yeah. See, there's this woman in Chicago, and I'm in love with her. I want to be where she is, and as long as she's somewhere with water I can have a business there, so I'm ready to follow her anywhere she goes."

I'm not expecting it when she launches herself at me. I topple back onto the bench, her weight on me in all the right places.

She kisses me over and over until we've melted into one another, our lips, tongues, hands and legs meshed together in a vortex of heat and need.

"Princess," I finally say, tearing my lips from hers. "I think it's time to go below."

"Definitely," she says, a wicked smile on her face. I sit up, taking her with me until she's straddling my lap, pressing against the hard on I've been sporting for the last ten minutes.

"So, I take it that was a 'yes, please move to Chicago for me'?"

She giggles, rubbing her nose against mine. "Yes, please move to Chicago for me."

"You don't mind that I'm not a billionaire CFO anymore?" I ask, even though I know the answer.

"All I've ever wanted is you," she says. "When Niko was a billionaire I wanted him. Now that Niko is a small business owner I want him too. I'll always want you, Niko. No matter what. You're my one, and I love you."

My heart soars and I warm everywhere, as if the sun decided to shine on me alone.

"You're mine too, Princess. I can't wait to make a whole new set of rules with you."

We kiss once more before we go below to start on the rest of our lives.

THE END

About the Author

Selena Laurence is the USA Today Bestselling Author of Edgy Contemporary Romance. In 2014 she was awarded the Reader's Crown Award for Contemporary Romance of the Year.

Selena lives in the foothills of the Rocky Mountains with her kids, Mr. L, "Goldendoodle" and "Demon Cat." When she's not writing she can be found at soccer games and tennis matches, or one of her favorite coffee shops. Online, see her at all these places:

Email: author@selenalaurence.com,
Facebook: SelenaLaurenceRomanceAuthor,
Twitter: @selenalaurence,
Instagram: selenalaurence,
Website: http://www.selenalaurence.com.

Sign up for her monthly newsletter here:
http://bit.ly/1mtE0pJ

Selena is represented by Jessica Faust at BookEnds Literary.

31380566R00162

Made in the USA
San Bernardino, CA
08 March 2016